USA TODAY and bestselling and RITA®
Award–winning author **Marie Ferrarella**
has written more than two hundred and
fifty books for Mills & Boon, some under
the name Marie Nicole. Her romances
are beloved by fans worldwide. Visit her
website: marieferrarella.com.

THE FORTUNE MOST LIKELY TO...

MARIE FERRARELLA

MILLS & BOON

First published in Great Britain 2018
by Mills & Boon, an imprint of HarperCollins*Publishers*
1 London Bridge Street, London, SE1 9GF

Large Print edition 2018

© 2018 Harlequin Books S.A.

Special thanks and acknowledgement
are given to Marie Ferrarella for her contribution to
The Fortunes of Texas: The Rulebreakers continuity.

ISBN: 978-0-263-07306-5

3478288-5

To
Susan Litman,
with thanks
for her
patience.

PROLOGUE

IT WAS TIME that he finally faced up to it. He had never gotten over her.

Sitting on the sofa in his living room, Dr. Everett Fortunado frowned as he looked into the glass of expensive whiskey he was sipping. The single glass, two fingers, was his way of winding down. Not from a hectic day spent at his successful, thriving medical practice, but from the stress of terminating yet another less-than-stellar, stillborn relationship.

How many failed relationships did that make now? Ten? Twelve? He wasn't sure.

He'd honestly lost count a number of years ago.

Admittedly, the women in those incredibly short-lived relationships had all become interchangeable. Now that he thought about it, none of them had ever stood out in his mind. And, if he was being honest about it, Everett couldn't remember half their names.

As for their faces, well, if pressed, he could give a general description, but there again, nothing about any of them had left a lasting impression on his mind. Strictly speaking, he could probably pass one or more of them on the street and not recognize them at all.

A mirthless laugh passed his lips. At thirty-three he was way too young to be on the threshold of dementia. No, that wasn't the reason behind this so-called memory loss problem. If he were being entirely honest with himself, he thought, taking another long, bracing sip of whiskey, this cavalcade of women who had been parading through his life for the last thirteen years were only poor substitutes for the one woman who had ever really mattered to him.

The only woman he had ever been in love with.

The woman he had lost.

Lila Clark, the girl he'd known since forever and had barely been aware of until he suddenly *saw* her for the first time that day in Senior English class. Though a straight A student, Everett had found himself faltering when it came to English. Lila sat next to him in class and he'd turned to her for help. She was the one responsible for getting him through Senior English.

And somewhere along the line during all that tutoring, Lila had managed to make off with his heart. He was crazy about her and really excited when he found out that she felt the same way about him. Not long after that, they began making plans for their future together.

And then it had all blown up on him.

When he'd lost her, his parents had told him that it was all for the best. They had pointed out that he was too young to think about settling down. They wanted their brightest child to focus on his future and not squander his vast potential by marrying a girl from a working-class family just because he'd gotten her pregnant. To them it had been the oldest ploy in the world: a poor girl trapping a rich boy because of his sense of obligation.

But Lila really wasn't like that. And she hadn't trapped him. She'd walked out on him.

Everett sat on the sofa now, watching the light from the lone lamp in his living room play across the amber liquid in the chunky glass in his hand. He would've given anything if he could go back those thirteen years.

If he could have, he wouldn't have talked Lila into giving up their baby for adoption.

Because that one thing had been the beginning of the end for them.

He'd been at Lila's side in the delivery room and, even then, he kept telling her that they were doing the right thing. That they were too young to get married and raise this baby. That they could always have more kids "later."

Lila changed that night. Changed from the happy, bright-eyed, full-of-life young woman he'd fallen in love with to someone he no longer even knew.

And that was the look in her eyes when she raised them to his. Like she was looking at someone she didn't recognize.

Right after she left the hospital, Lila had told him she never wanted to see him again. He'd tried to reason with her, but she just wouldn't listen.

Lila had disappeared out of his life right after that.

Crushed, he'd gone back to college, focusing every bit of energy entirely on his studies.

He'd always wanted to be a doctor, ever since he was a little boy, and that became his lifeline after Lila left. He clung to it to the exclusion of everything else.

And it had paid off, he thought now, raising his almost-empty glass in a silent toast to his thriving career. He was a doctor. A highly successful, respected doctor. His career was booming.

Conversely, his personal life was in the dumpster.

Everett sighed. If he had just said, "Let's keep the baby," everything would have been different. And his life wouldn't have felt so empty every time he walked into his house.

He wouldn't have felt so empty.

Blowing out a breath, Everett rose from the sofa and walked over to the liquor cabinet. Normally, he restricted himself to just one drink, but tonight was different. It was the anniversary of the day Lila had ended their relationship. He could be forgiven a second drink.

At least, he told himself, he could fill his empty glass, if not his life.

CHAPTER ONE

"YOUR PROBLEM, BROTHER DEAR," Schuyler said after having listened to him tell her that maybe he'd made a mistake talking Lila into giving up their baby all those years ago, "is that you think too much. You're always overthinking things and making yourself crazy in the process."

"Says the woman who always led with her heart," Everett commented.

"And that seems to be working out for me, doesn't it?" Schuyler asked.

He could hear the broad smile in her voice. It all but throbbed through the phone. Everett had no response for that. All he could do at the moment was sigh. Sigh and feel just a little bit jealous because his little sister had found something that he was beginning to think he never would find again: love.

"By thinking so much back then about how everything would affect your future," Schuyler went on, "I think you blew it with Lila. You were so focused on your future, on becoming a doctor, that you just couldn't see how badly she felt about giving up her baby—*your* baby," she emphasized. "And because you didn't notice, didn't seem to feel just as badly as she did about the adoption, you broke Lila's heart. If it were me, I would have never forgiven someone for breaking my heart that way," Schuyler told him.

"Thanks for being so supportive," Everett said sarcastically.

This was *not* why he'd called his sister, why he'd lowered his guard and allowed himself to be so vulnerable. Maybe he should have known better, he thought, about to terminate the call.

"I *am* being supportive," Schuyler insisted. "I'm just calling it the way I see it. I love you, Ev, and you know I'm always on your side. But I know you. I don't want you to get your hopes up that if you just approach her, she'll fly back into your arms and everything'll be just the way it was back then. Not after thirteen years and *not* after what went down between the two of you back then. Trust me, Lila is not going to get back together with you that easily."

"I know that and I don't want to get back together with Lila," he insisted defensively. "I just want to talk to her." Everett paused because this next thing was hard for him to say, even to Schuyler, someone he had always trusted implicitly. Lowering his voice, he told his sister, "Maybe even apologize to her for the way things ended between us back then."

He could tell from Schuyler's voice that she felt for him. But she was far from optimistic about the outcome of all this. "Look, Everett, I know that your heart's in the right place, but I really don't want to see it stomped on."

"No worries," Everett assured her. "My heart is not as vulnerable as you think."

What he'd just said might have been a lie, but if it was, it was a lie he was telling himself as well as his sister.

He had a feeling that Schuyler saw it that way too because he could hear the skepticism in her voice as she said, just before she ended their call, "Well, I wish you luck with that. Maybe Lila'll listen to reason."

* * *

Maybe.

The single word seemed to throb in his head as Everett decided to find out as much as he could about Lila and what she was doing these days.

It had all started two months ago when he'd taken the day off, gotten another doctor to cover for him and had driven the 165 miles from Houston to Austin to pick up his sister, Schuyler. At the time, he was supposed to be bringing Schuyler back home.

Given to acting on impulse, his younger sister had initially gone to Austin because she had gotten it into her head to track down Nathan Fortune. The somewhat reclusive man was supposedly her cousin and the ever-inquisitive Schuyler was looking for answers about their family tree. The current thinking was that she and the rest of their brothers and sisters were all possibly related to the renowned Fortune family.

It was while Schuyler was looking for those answers that she decided to get closer to the Mendoza family whose history was intertwined with the Fortunes. She managed to get so close to one of them—Carlo Mendoza—that she wound up completely losing her heart to him.

Confused, unsure of herself for very possibly the first time in her life, Schuyler had turned to the one person she was closest to.

She'd called Everett.

Listening to his sister pouring out her heart—and citing her all uncertainties, not just about her genealogy investigation but about the direction her heart had gone in—he had decided he needed to see Schuyler and maybe convince her to come home.

But Schuyler had reconciled with her man and decided to stay in Austin after all. Everett returned home without her. But he hadn't come away completely empty-handed. What Everett had come home with was a renewed sense of having made a terrible mistake thirteen years ago. And that had come about because while he'd been in Austin, he had run into Lila.

Sort of.

He saw Lila entering a sandwich shop and it had been a jarring experience for him. It had instantly propelled him back through time and just like that, all the old feelings had come rushing back to him, saturating him like a huge tidal wave. At least they had in his case. However, he'd been struck by the aura of sadness he detected about her. A sadness that had *not* been there when they were in high school together.

He'd thought—hoped really—that when he got back to Houston, back to his practice, he'd be able to drive thoughts of Lila back into the past where they belonged. Instead, they began to haunt him, vividly pushing their way into his dreams at night, sneaking up on him during the day whenever he had an unguarded moment.

He began wondering in earnest about what had happened to her in all those years since they'd been together. And that sadness he'd detected—was *he* responsible for that? Or was there some other reason for its existence?

He felt compelled to find out.

Like everyone else of his generation, Everett turned to social media in his quest for information about Lila Clark.

He found her on Facebook.

When he saw that Lila had listed herself as "single" and that there were only a few photographs posted on her page, mainly from vacation spots she had visited, he felt somewhat heartened.

Maybe, a little voice in his head whispered, it wasn't too late to make amends after all.

Damn it, Everett, get hold of yourself. This is exactly what Schuyler warned you about. Don't get your hopes up, at least not until you talk to Lila again and exchange more than six words with her.

Who knows, she might have changed and you won't even like Lila 2.0.

Everett struggled to talk himself out of letting his imagination take flight. He tried to get himself to go slow—or maybe not go at all.

But the latter was just not an option.

He knew he felt too strongly about this, too highly invested in righting a wrong he'd committed in the past. Now that he'd made up his mind about the matter, he needed to make Lila understand that he regretted the way things had gone thirteen years ago.

Regretted not being more emotionally supportive of her.

Regretted not being able to see the daughter they had *both* lost.

Still, he continued to try to talk himself out of it for two days after he found Lila on Facebook. Tried to make himself just walk away from the whole idea: from getting in contact with her, from apologizing and making amends. All of it.

But he couldn't.

So finally, on the evening of the third day, Everett sat down in front of his computer, powered up his internet connection and pulled up Facebook. Specifically, he pulled up Lila's profile.

He'd stared at it for a full ten minutes before he finally began to type a message to her.

Hi, Lila. It's been a long time. I'm planning on being in Austin soon. Let's have lunch together and do some catching up. I'd really welcome the chance to see and talk with you.

Those four simple sentences took him close to half an hour to settle on. He must have written and deleted thirty sentences before he finally decided on those. Then it took him another ten minutes before he sent those four sweated-over sentences off into cyberspace.

For the next two hours he checked on that page close to a dozen and a half times, all without any luck. He was about to power down his computer for the night when he pulled up Lila's Facebook page one last time.

"She answered," he announced out loud even though there was no one around to hear him.

Sitting down in his chair, he read Lila's response, unconsciously savoring each word as if it was a precious jewel.

If you're going to be here Friday, I can meet you for lunch at 11:30. I just need to warn you that I only get forty-five minutes for lunch, so our meeting will be short. We're usually really swamped where I work.

Everett could hardly believe that she'd actually agreed to meet with him. He'd been half prepared to read her rejection. Whistling, he immediately posted a response.

11:30 on Friday sounds great. Since I'm unfamiliar with Austin, you pick the place and let me know.

After sleeping fitfully, he decided to get up early. He had a full slate of appointments that day. Best to get a jump on it. But the minute he passed the computer, he knew what he had to do first.

And there, buried amid approximately forty other missives—all of which were nothing short of junk mail—was Lila's response. All she'd written was the name of a popular chain of restaurants, followed by its address. But his heart soared.

Their meeting was set.

If he'd been agile enough to pull it off, Everett would have leaped up and clicked his heels together.

As it was, he got ready for work very quickly and left the house within the half hour—singing.

The second Lila hit the send button on Facebook, she immediately regretted it.

What am I thinking? she upbraided herself. Was she crazy? Did she actually *want* to meet with someone who had so carelessly broken her heart? Who was responsible for the single most heart-wrenching event to have happened in her life?

"What's wrong with you? Are you hell-bent on being miserable?" she asked herself as she walked away from her computer. It was after eleven o'clock at night and she was alone.

The way she was on most nights.

Maybe that was the problem, Lila told herself. She was tired of being alone and when she'd seen that message from Everett on her Facebook page, it had suddenly stirred up a lot of old memories.

"Memories you're better off forgetting, remember?" she demanded.

But they weren't all bad, she reminded herself. As a matter of fact, if she thought back, a lot of those memories had been good.

Very good.

For a large chunk of her Senior year and a portion of her first year at community college, Everett had been the love of her life. He'd made her happier than she could ever remember being.

But it was what had happened at the end that outweighed everything, that threw all those good recollections into the shadows, leaving her to remember that awful, awful ache in her heart as Emma was taken out of her arms and she watched her baby being carried away.

Away from her.

She'd wanted Everett to hold her then. To tell her that he was aching as much as she was. That he felt as if something had been torn away from his heart, too, the way she felt it had for her.

But all he had said was: "It's for the best." As if there was something that could be described as "best" about never being able to see your baby again. A baby that had been conceived in love and embodied the two of them in one tiny little form.

Lila felt tears welling up in her eyes even after all this time, felt them spilling out even though she'd tried hard to squeeze them back.

She wished she hadn't agreed to see Everett.

But if she'd said no to lunch, Everett would have probably put two and two together and realized that she hadn't the courage to see him again.

If she'd turned him down, he would've understood just how much he still mattered to her.

No, Lila told herself, she had no way out. She *had* to see him again. Had to sit there across from him at a table, making inane conversation and proving to him that he meant nothing to her.

That would be her ultimate revenge for his having so wantonly, so carelessly, ripped out her heart without so much as a moment's pause or a word of actual genuine comfort.

"We'll have lunch, Everett," she said, addressing his response that was posted on her Facebook page. "We'll have lunch, and then you'll realize just what you lost all those years ago. Lost forever. Because I was the very best thing that could have ever happened to you," she added with finality.

Her words rang hollow to her ear.

It didn't matter, she told herself. She had a couple of days before she had to meet with him. A couple of days to practice making herself sound as if she believed every syllable she uttered.

She'd have it letter-perfect by the time they met, she promised herself.

She *had* to.

CHAPTER TWO

HALF THE CONTENTS of Lila's closet was now spread out all over her bed. She spent an extra hour going through each item slowly before finally making up her mind.

Lila dressed with great care, selecting a two-piece gray-blue outfit that flattered her curves as well as sharply bringing out the color of her eyes.

Ordinarily, putting on makeup entailed a dash of lipstick for Lila, if that. This morning she highlighted her eyes, using both mascara and a little eye shadow. She topped it off with a swish of blush to accent her high cheekbones, smoothed her long auburn hair, then sprayed just the slightest bit of perfume.

Finished, she slowly inspected herself from all angles in her wardrobe mirror before she decided that she was ready to confront a past she'd thought she'd buried—and in so doing, make Dr. Everett Fortunado eat his heart out.

Maybe, Lila thought as she left her house, if she took this much trouble getting ready for the occasional dates she went out on, she might not still be single at the age of thirty-three.

Lila sighed. She knew better. It wasn't her clothes or her makeup that were responsible for her single status.

It was her.

After breaking up with Everett, she had picked herself up and dusted herself off. In an all-out attempt to totally reinvent herself, Lila had left Houston and moved to Austin where no one knew her or anything about the past she was determined to forget and put totally behind her.

She'd gone to work at the Fortune Foundation, a nonprofit organization dedicated to providing assistance to the needy. Through hard work, she'd swiftly risen and was now manager of her department.

And because of her work, Lila's life went from intolerable to good. At least her professional life did.

Her personal life, however, was another story.

Sure, she'd dated. She'd tried blind dates as well as online dating. She'd joined clubs and had gone to local sporting events to cheer on the home team. She'd gone out with rich men as well as poor ones and those in-between.

It wasn't that Lila couldn't meet a man, she just couldn't meet *the* man.

And probably even if she could, she thought, that still wouldn't have done the trick. Because no matter who she went out with, she couldn't trust him.

Everett had destroyed her ability to trust any man she might become involved with.

Try as she might, she couldn't lower her guard. She just couldn't bear to have a repeat performance of what had happened to her with Everett.

Rather than risk that, she kept her heart firmly under lock and key. And that guaranteed a life of loneliness.

At this point in her life, Lila had decided to give up looking for Mr. Right. Instead, she forced herself to embrace being Stubbornly Single.

As she took one last look in the mirror and

walked out the door, she told herself that was what she really wanted.

One day she might convince herself that was true.

Her upgraded appearance did not go unnoticed when she walked into the office at the Fortune Foundation that morning.

"Well, someone looks extra nice today," Lucie Fortune Chesterfield Parker noted the moment that Lila crossed the threshold. "Do you have a hot date tonight?" she asked as she made her way over toward Lila.

"No, I don't," Lila answered, hoping that would be the end of it.

Belatedly, she thought that maybe she should have brought this outfit with her and changed in the ladies' room before going to lunch instead of coming in dressed like this.

Lucie and she were friends and had been almost from the very first time they met at the Foundation, but Lila really didn't want to talk about the man she was having lunch with.

Initially from England, Lucie was married to Chase Parker, a Texas oil heir who had been her teenage sweetheart. Because of that, Lucie considered herself to be an expert on romance and she felt she had great radar when it came to the subject.

Her radar was apparently on red alert now as she swiftly looked Lila over.

Studying her, Lucie repeated, "Not tonight?"

"No," Lila said firmly. She never broke stride, determined to get to her office and close the door on this subject—literally as well as figuratively.

"Lunch, then?" Lucie pressed. "You certainly didn't get all dolled up like that for us."

Lila looked at her sharply over her shoulder, but her coworker didn't back off. The expression on her face indicated that she thought she was onto something.

When Lila made no response, Lucie pressed harder. "Well, *are* you going to lunch with someone?"

Lila wanted to say no and be done with it. She was, after all, a private person and no one here knew about her past. She'd never shared any of it. No about the child she'd given up for adoption or the man who had broken her heart. However, it wasn't in her to lie and even if it were, Lucie was as close to a real friend as she had in Austin. She didn't want to risk alienating her if the truth ever happened to come out—which it might, likely at the most inopportune time.

So after a moment of soul-searching, she finally answered Lucie's question.

"Yes."

Lucie looked at her more closely, obviously intrigued. "Anyone I know?" she asked.

"No," Lila answered automatically.

Not anyone I know, either. Not really, Lila silently added. After all, it had been thirteen years since she'd last been with Everett. And besides, how well had she known him back then anyway? He certainly hadn't behaved the way she'd expected him to. It made her think that maybe she had never really known Everett Fortunado at all.

"Where did you meet him?" Lucie wanted to know, apparently hungry for details about her friend's lunch date.

"Why all the questions?" Lila reached her office, but unfortunately it was situated right next to Lucie's. Both offices were enclosed in glass, allowing them to easily see one another over the course of the day.

"Because you're my friend and I'm curious," Lucie answered breezily. "You've practically become a workaholic these last couple of months, hardly coming up for air. That doesn't leave you much time for socializing."

Pausing by her doorway, Lila blew out a breath. "It's someone I knew back in high school," she answered. She stuck close to the truth. There was less chance for error that way. "He's in town on business for a couple of days. He looked me up on Facebook and he suggested having lunch to catch up, so I said yes."

Lila walked over to her desk, really hoping that would be the end of it. But apparently it wasn't because Lucie didn't retreat to her own office. Her friend remained standing in Lila's doorway, looking at her as if she was attempting to carefully dissect every word out of her mouth.

"How well did you know this guy—back in high school, I mean?" Lucie asked, tacking on the few words after a small beat.

Lila stood there feeling as if she was under a microscope.

Did it show, she wondered. Did Lucie suspect that there had been more than just high school between her and Everett?

"Why?" she asked suspiciously, wondering what Lucie was getting at. It wasn't that she didn't trust Lucie, it was just that inherently she had trouble lowering her guard around *anyone*.

"Well, if someone who I knew back in high school suddenly turned up in my life," Lucie said easily, "I don't think I'd dress up in something that would make me look like a runway model just to go out to lunch with him."

Lila shrugged, avoiding Lucie's eyes. "I'm just showing off the trappings of a successful career, I guess."

"Are you sure that's all it is?" Lucie asked, observing her closely.

Lila raised her chin, striking almost a defiant pose. "I'm sure," she answered.

Lucie inclined her head, accepting her friend's story. "Well, if I were you, I'd remember to take a handkerchief with me."

Lila stared at the other woman. What Lucie had just said made absolutely no sense to her.

"Why?"

Lucie's smile was a wide one, tinged in amusement. "Because you'll need a handkerchief to wipe up your friend's drool once he gets a load of you looking like that."

Lila looked down at herself. Granted, she'd taken a lot of time choosing what to wear, but it was still just a two-piece outfit. "I don't look any different than I usually do," Lila protested.

Lucie's smile widened a little more as she turned to leave. "Okay, if you say so," she answered agreeably, going along with Lila's version. "But between you and me, you look like a real knockout."

Good, Lila thought. That was the look she was going for.

There were mornings at work when the minutes would just seem to drag by, behaving as if lunchtime would never come. Lila would have given anything for that sort of a morning this time around because today, the minutes just seemed to race by, until suddenly, before she knew it, the clock on the wall opposite her office said it was eleven fifteen.

She'd told Everett that she would meet him at the restaurant she'd selected at eleven thirty.

That meant it was time for her to get going.

Lila took a deep breath, pushed her chair away from her desk and got up.

When she stood up, her hands braced against her desk, her legs felt as if they had suddenly lost the power of mobility.

For a moment, it was as if she was rooted in place.

This was ridiculous, Lila told herself, getting her purse from her drawer.

She closed the drawer a little too hard. The sound reverberated through the glass walls and next door Lucie immediately looked in her direction. Grinning, Lucie gave her a thumbs-up sign.

Lila forced herself to smile in response then, concentrating as hard as she could, she managed to get her frozen legs moving. She wanted to be able to leave the office before Lucie thought to stick her head in to say something.

Or ask something.

This was all going to be over with soon, Lila promised herself.

Once out of the building, she made her way

to her car. An hour and she'd be back, safe and sound in the office and this so-called "lunch date" would be behind her, Lila thought, trying to think positive thoughts.

It would be behind her and she'd never have to see Everett again.

But first, she pointedly reminded herself, she *was* going to have to get through this ordeal. She was going to have to sit at a table, face Everett and pretend that everything was just fine.

She was going to have to pretend that the past was just that: the past, and that it had nothing to do with the present. Pretend that those events from thirteen years ago didn't affect her any longer and definitely didn't get in the way of her eating and enjoying her lunch. Pretend that the memory of those events didn't impede her swallowing, or threaten to make her too sick to keep her food down.

Reaching her car, Lila got in and then just sat there, willing herself to start it. Willing herself to drive over to the restaurant and get this lunch over with.

Not a good plan, Lila. This is not a good plan. You should have never agreed to have lunch with Everett. When he wrote to you on your Facebook page, asking to meet with you, you should have told him to go to hell and stay there.

You've got no one to blame but yourself for this.

Lila let out a shaky breath and then glanced up into the rearview mirror.

Lucie was right. She looked fantastic.

Go and make him eat his heart out, Lila silently ordered herself. *And then, after you've finished eating and he asks if he could see you again, you tell him No!*

You tell him no, she silently repeated.

Taking another deep breath, she turned the key in the ignition.

The car rumbled to life. After another moment and a few more words of encouragement to herself, Lila pulled out of her parking space and drove out of the parking structure and off the lot.

The restaurant she'd selected was normally barely a five-minute drive away from the Foundation. Even with the sluggish midday traffic, it only took her ten minutes to get there. Before she knew it, she was pulling into a space in the restaurant's parking lot.

Sitting there, thinking of what was ahead of her, Lila found that she had to psych herself up in order to leave the shelter of her vehicle and walk into the restaurant.

To face her past.

"No," she contradicted herself through gritted teeth. "Not to face the past. To finally shut the door on it once and for all and start your future."

Yes, she had a life and a career, a career she was quite proud of. But she also needed to cut all ties to the woman she had once been. That starry-eyed young woman who thought that love lasted forever and that she had found her true love. That woman had to, quite simply, be put to rest once and for all.

And she intended to do that by having lunch with Everett, the man who had taken her heart and made mincemeat out of it. And once lunch was done, she was going to tell him goodbye one last time. Tell him goodbye and make him realize that she meant it.

Lila slowly got out of her car and then locked it.

Squaring her shoulders, she headed for the restaurant. It was time to beard the lion in his den and finally be set free.

CHAPTER THREE

THIS WAS ABSURD, Everett thought. He was a well-respected, sought-after physician who had graduated from medical school at the top of his class. Skilled and exceedingly capable. Yet here he was, sitting in a restaurant, feeling as nervous as a teenager waiting for his first date to walk in.

This was Lila for God's sake, he lectured himself. Lila, someone he'd once believed was his soul mate. Lila, whom he'd once been closer to than anyone else in the world and had loved with his whole heart and soul. There was absolutely no reason for him to be tapping the table with his long fingers and fidgeting like some inexperienced kid.

Yet here he was, half an hour ahead of time, watching the door when he wasn't watching the clock, waiting for Lila to walk in.

Wondering if she wouldn't.

Wondering if, for some reason, she would

wind up changing her mind at the last minute and call him to cancel their lunch. Or worse, not call at all.

Why am I doing this to myself? Everett silently demanded. Why was he making himself crazy like this? So what if she didn't show? It wouldn't be the end of the world. At least, no more than it was all those years ago when Lila had told him she didn't ever want to see him again.

The words had stung back then and he hadn't known what to do with himself, how to think, what to say. In time, he'd calmed down, started to think rationally again. He had decided to stay away from her for a while, thinking that Lila would eventually come to her senses and change her mind.

Except that, when he finally went to see her, he found out that she was gone. Lila had taken off for parts unknown and no one knew where. Or, if they did know, no one was telling him no matter how much he asked.

That was when his parents had sat him down and told him that it was all for the best. They reminded him that he had a destiny to fulfill and now he was free to pursue that destiny.

Not having anything else to cling to, he threw himself into his studies and did exactly what was expected of him—and more.

He did all that only to end up here, sitting in an Austin restaurant, watching the door and praying each time it opened that it was Lila coming in and walking back into his life.

But each time, it wasn't Lila who walked in.

Until it was.

Everett felt his pulse leap up with a jolt the second he saw her. All these years and she had only gotten more beautiful.

He immediately rose in his seat, waving to catch her attention. He had to stop himself from calling out her name, instinctively knowing that would embarrass her. They weren't teenagers anymore.

Lila had almost turned around at the door just before she opened it. It was only the fact that she would have been severely disappointed in herself for acting like such a coward that forced her to come inside.

The second she did, she immediately saw Everett and then it was too late to run for cover. Too late to change her mind.

The game was moving forward.

She forced a smile to her lips despite the fact that her stomach was tied in a knot so tight she could hardly breathe. It was the sort of smile that strangers gave one another in an attempt to break the ice. Except that there was no breaking the ice that she felt in her soul as she looked at Everett.

All the old heartache came rushing back to her in spades.

"I'm sorry," she murmured to Everett when she finally reached the table. "Am I late?"

"No," he quickly assured her. "I'm early. I didn't know if there was going to be a lot of traffic, or if I'd have trouble finding this place, so I left the hotel early." A sheepish smile curved his lips. "As it turned out, there was no traffic and the restaurant was easy enough to find."

"That's good," she responded, already feeling at a loss as to what to say next.

She was about to sit down and Everett quickly came around the table to hold out her chair for her.

"Thank you," she murmured, feeling even more awkward as she took her seat.

Having pushed her chair in for her, Everett circled back to his own and sat down opposite her. He could feel his heart swelling just to look at her.

"You look really great," Everett told her with enthusiasm.

Again she forced a quick smile to her lips. "Thank you," she murmured.

At least all that time she'd spent this morning fussing with her makeup and searching for the right thing to wear had paid off, she thought. Looking good, she had once heard, was the best revenge. She wanted Everett to be aware of what he'd given up. She wanted him to feel at least a little pang over having so carelessly lost her.

The years had been kind to him, as well, she reluctantly admitted. His six-foot frame had filled in well, though he was still taut and lean, and his dark hair framed a handsome, manly face and highlighted his dark-blue eyes. Eyes that seemed to be studying her.

"But you do seem a little...different some-how," Everett said quietly a moment later.

She wasn't sure what he meant by that and it marred her triumph just a little. Was that a veiled criticism, she wondered.

"Well, it has been thirteen years," she reminded Everett stiffly. "We knew each other a long time ago. That is," she qualified, "if we ever really knew each other at all."

He looked at her, wondering if that was a dig or if he was just being extremely touchy.

It seemed there were four of them at the table. The people they were now and the ghosts of the people they had been thirteen years ago.

The moment stretched out, becoming more uncomfortable. "What's that supposed to mean?" Everett asked her.

"Just an observation," Lila answered casually. "Who really knows who they are at that young an age?" she asked philosophically. "I know that I didn't."

He sincerely doubted that. "Oh, I think you did," Everett told her.

Seeing the server approaching, she held her reply. When the server asked if he could start them out with a drink, Lila ordered a glass of sparkling water rather than anything alcoholic. Everett followed her example and asked for the same.

"And if you don't mind, I'd like to order now,"

Lila told the young server. "I have to be getting back to the office soon," she explained.

"Of course."

After he took their orders and left, Everett picked up the thread of their conversation. "I think you knew just what you wanted years ago," he told her. "I'm the one who got it all wrong."

Was he saying that out of pity for her, she wondered, feeling her temper beginning to rise as her stomach churned.

"On the contrary," Lila responded. "You were the only kid who was serious when he said he wanted to play 'doctor.' If you ask me, 'Dr. Fortunado' achieved everything he ever dreamed about as a kid."

Everett's eyes met hers. Longing and sadness for all the lost years filled him. For the time being, he disregarded the note of bitterness he thought he detected in her voice.

"Not everything," he told her.

This was an act. She wasn't going to fall for it, Lila thought, grateful that the server picked that moment to return with their drinks and their orders. Everett wasn't fooling her. He was just saying that so that she would forget about the past. Forget her pain.

As if that were remotely possible.

Silence stretched out between them. Everett shifted uncomfortably.

"So, tell me about you," he finally urged. "What are you doing these days?"

Lila pushed around the lettuce in her salad as if the fate of the world depended on just the right placement. She kept her eyes on her plate as she spoke, deliberately avoiding making any further eye contact with him. She had always loved Everett's dark blue eyes. When they'd been together, she felt she could easily get lost in those eyes of his and happily drown.

Now she couldn't bear to look into them.

"I'm a manager of one of the departments at the Fortune Foundation. My work involves health outreach programs for the poorer families living in the Austin area."

That sounded just like her, Everett thought. Lila was always trying to help others.

But something else she'd said caught his attention. "Did you say the Fortune Foundation?"

"Yes," she answered. Suspicion entered

her voice as she eyed him closely and asked, "Why?"

"Well, it just seems funny that you should mention the Fortunes. My family just recently found out that our last name might very well be 'Fortune' rather than 'Fortunado.'" He pulled his face into a grin. "Crazy coincidence, isn't it?"

Coincidence. Lila had another word for it. Her eyes narrowed as she pinned him with a look. "Is that why you wanted to get together for lunch?" she wanted to know. "To ask me questions about the Fortunes and see how much information you could get?"

He stared at her, practically dumbstruck. What was she talking about?

"The fact that you work for the Fortune Foundation has absolutely nothing to do with my wanting to get together with you," Everett insisted. Thinking over her accusation, he shook his head. "I'm not even sure if the family *is* connected to the Fortunes. It could all just be a silly rumor or a hoax.

"And even if it *does* turn out to actually be true, my family's not positive if we want to reveal the connection. It sounds like there are a lot of skeletons in the Fortune closet. Actually," he confessed, backtracking, "maybe I spoke out of turn, talking about the possible connection. I'd appreciate it if you didn't say anything to anyone at the Foundation."

Did he think she was going to go running back after lunch and act like a human recording device, spilling every word that had been said between them? Just what sort of an image did he have of her?

Lila found herself struggling to tamp down her temper before she said anything.

"Well, obviously not everyone at the Foundation is a Fortune," she pointed out icily. "And anyway, the Fortunes are a huge family. I don't think anyone would be surprised to find out that there's another branch or two out there. There've been so many that have been uncovered already."

Everett nodded. "Makes sense," he agreed, even though he still felt a little leery about having the story spread around that the Fortunados believed that they were really Fortunes. Trying to steer the conversation in a different direction, he asked, "I'm curious—what do you think of the Fortunes?"

Lila's smile was reserved. She remembered hearing a great many unnerving rumors concerning the Fortune family before she began working at the Foundation. But most of what she'd been told turned out not to be true. For the most part, the stories were just run-of-the-mill gossip spread by people who were jealous of the family's success as well as their money.

"In my experience," she qualified in case he wanted to challenge her words, "they're a great family. A lot of people hold the fact that they're rich against them, but the family does a lot of good with that money. The Fortunes I've met aren't power hungry or self-centered. A great many of them have devoted their lives to the Foundation, to doing as much good as they can," she emphasized.

"Power-hungry and self-centered," Everett repeated the words that she had used. "Is that the way you think of most rich people?" he asked. Then, before Lila could answer, he went on to ask her another question—the question he *really* wanted the answer to. "Is that how you think of me?"

Her eyes narrowed again as she looked at Everett intently. Rather than answering his question, she turned it around and asked Everett a question of her own. "Did I say that?" she asked pointedly.

"No," he was forced to admit. She hadn't said it in so many words, but he felt that Lila had implied it by the way she'd structured her sentence.

"Then let's leave it at that, shall we?" Lila told him.

It was obvious to Everett that he was going to have one hell of a rough road ahead of him if he ever hoped to win her over. And despite what he had told his sister to the contrary, he really did want to win Lila back.

He admitted to himself that Lila was the missing ingredient in his life, the reason that every triumph he had had felt so hollow, so empty. It felt that way because Lila wasn't there to share it with him.

For now, he changed the subject to something lighter. "You know," he said as he watched Lila make short work of her Caesar salad, "as a doctor I should tell you that eating your food that fast is really not good for your digestion."

"And being late getting back from lunch

isn't good for my job approval," Lila countered tersely. Finished, she retired her fork.

Was she really serious about needing to get back so quickly? Initially, he'd thought it was just an excuse, a way to terminate their meeting if she felt it wasn't going well. Now she seemed to be waving it in front of her like a flag at the end of a marathon.

"I thought you said that you were the manager of your department."

"I am. And as manager, it's up to me to set a good example," she told him.

If she really wanted to leave, Everett thought, he couldn't very well stop her. "Can't argue with that, I guess."

"No, you can't," she informed him, a stubborn look in her eyes as they met his.

He gave it one last try. "I suppose this means that you don't want to order dessert. I remember that you used to love desserts of all kinds," he recalled.

"I did," she acknowledged. "But then I grew up," she told him crisply. "And right now, I'm afraid I have no time for dessert."

He nodded. "Maybe next time, then."

Lila was about to murmur the obligatory, "It was good seeing you again," but his words stopped her cold. "Next time?" she echoed, surprised and stunned.

She sounded far from happy about the prospect. Everett did his best to ignore the coolness in her voice. Instead, he explained his comment. "I might be spending more time in Austin over the next few months."

"Oh?" She could feel the walls going up around her. Walls meant to protect her. She could feel herself struggling with the strong desire to run for the hills. She forced herself not to move a muscle. "Why?"

"Well, with Schuyler engaged to Carlo Mendoza and living here, I thought I'd be the good brother and visit her from time to time to make her transition here a little easier for her." This was harder than he thought it would be and it took him a few moments before he finally said, "I was wondering if it's all right with you if I call you the next time I'm in Austin."

His question was met with silence.

CHAPTER FOUR

DESPITE THE FACT that the restaurant was enjoying a healthy amount of business with most of the tables taken, the silence at their table seemed to wrap tightly around Everett and Lila.

Lila realized that Everett was waiting for her to answer him. And unfortunately, the floor hadn't opened up and swallowed her, so she was forced to say *something*. At a loss and wanting to stall until something came to her, Lila played dumb.

Clearing her throat she asked, "Excuse me? What did you say?"

Everett had a sinking feeling in the pit of his stomach as he repeated, "I asked if it would be all right with you if I called you the next time I was in Austin. You know, so we could get together again," he added and then watched her, waiting for an answer.

Again? Lila thought, astonished. *I'm barely surviving this time.*

She debated just shrugging her shoulders and saying, "Sure," with the hopes that if and when Everett called, she would have been able to come up with some sort of a viable excuse why she couldn't see him again.

But if she didn't put him off now, there was the very real possibility that she'd be doomed to go through another uncomfortable meeting in the near future.

Gathering her courage, Lila told him, "Um, I'm not sure if that's such a good idea."

If he were being honest with himself, Everett had half expected her to react this way. Still, actually *hearing* Lila say the words was very difficult for him.

Nodding grimly at her rebuff, he told her, "I understand."

But he really didn't understand because he didn't think it was a bad idea. He thought it was a perfectly *good* idea, one that would allow him another chance to convince her that they should try making their relationship work again after all these years.

Because they *belonged* together.

"Well, I really need to get going," she told Everett, rising to her feet. When he began to do the same, she quickly said, "Oh, don't leave on my account. Stay," she urged. "Have that dessert," she added. And then she concluded coldly, "I wish you luck with the rest of your life."

Then, turning on her heel, she quickly left the restaurant without so much as a backward glance.

Lila didn't exhale until the restaurant doors closed behind her.

Her heart was hammering hard and the brisk walk to her car had nothing to do with it. Lila didn't come anywhere close to relaxing until she reached her vehicle and got in.

Then she released her breath slowly.

She'd done it, she thought. She'd survived seeing him again.

She really hoped that Everett hadn't realized just how affected she was by his presence. With that in mind, there was just no way she could see him again, Lila thought. She was certain that she wouldn't be able to endure being face-to-face with Everett a second time, even if it was only for a couple of minutes.

But she'd done it. Lila silently congratulated herself as she started up her car. She'd sat across from Everett Fortunado and she hadn't bolted. She'd held her ground until she announced that she had to be getting back.

And now, having made it through that and gotten it out of the way, she could go on with the rest of her life.

Everett left the restaurant a couple of minutes after Lila did. There seemed to be no point in staying. He'd only mentioned having dessert because he remembered how fond of sweets she had always been. The thought of dessert had no allure for him, especially now that Lila had left. So he paid the tab and walked out.

He had barely managed to get into his car and buckle up before his cell phone rang. His first thought when he heard the phone was that it was Lila, calling to say she had changed her mind about having him call her the next time he was in Austin.

But when he answered the phone, it wasn't Lila. It was Schuyler.

"So how was it?" his sister asked in lieu of a hello.

Trying hard not to sound irritated, he asked her, "Why are you calling? I could have still been at the restaurant with Lila."

"I took a chance," she told him. "If you were still with Lila, I figured you wouldn't have answered your cell. But you did," she concluded with a resigned sigh. "So I take it that she really did have a short lunch break."

He didn't have it in him to lie or make something up, so he just said vaguely, "Something like that."

He should have known Schuyler wanted to know more. "What was it like *exactly*?" she asked him.

Everett sighed. There was no point in playing games or pretending that everything was fine. He'd been pretending that for the last thirteen years and it had just brought him to this painful moment of truth. And he knew that Schuyler would just keep after him until he told about lunch.

"I think Lila might hate me," he said to his

sister. He'd said "might" because stating it flatly just hurt too much.

"Hate you?" Schuyler questioned in surprise. "Why? What happened at lunch?" Then she chuckled. "Did she try to set you on fire?"

Everett laughed dryly. "No, she stopped short of that. But when I asked if I could call her again the next time I was in Austin, she told me she didn't think that was such a good idea."

"Wait, back up," Schuyler told her brother. "You *asked* her if you could call?"

"Yes." Schuyler was making it sound like he'd done something bad, but he had just been trying to be thoughtful of Lila's feelings. He didn't want Lila thinking he just presumed things. He was proud of the fact that he was first and foremost a gentleman.

He heard his sister sigh in disbelief. "Everett, you are a brilliant, brilliant doctor and probably the smartest man I know, but what you know about women could be stuffed into a walnut shell with room for a wad of chewing gum. You don't *ask* a woman if you can call her. You just call her."

He didn't operate like that. "What if she doesn't want me to call?"

"Then you'll find that out *after* the fact," Schuyler told him. "Believe me, if she doesn't want you to call, she'll let you know when she answers the phone. But if you hold off calling because she said she doesn't want you to, then you might wind up missing out on an opportunity."

This was making his head hurt. "Nothing is straightforward with you women, is it?"

"That's where the aura of mystery comes in," Schuyler told him with a laugh. And then her voice sobered. "*Are* you planning on seeing Lila again?"

Lila had as good as told him not to—but he couldn't bring himself to go along with that. Not yet. Not while he felt that there might be the slimmest chance to change her mind.

"I'm going to try," he confessed.

"When?" Schuyler questioned. "Now?"

"No." He was still smarting from Lila's rejection. "I think I'm going to give her a little time to mull things over. I'll probably talk with her the next time I'm in Austin."

"Talk with her about what?" Schuyler wanted to know.

"I want to make things right," Everett explained simply. "Maybe even tell her—"

Schuyler cut him off before he could say anything further. "Ev, not even *you* can bring back the past, you know that, right?"

"Yes, I know that," he said impatiently, "but I just want Lila to know that I wish I'd handled things differently back them. Schuyler, you have your happy ending in the works," he pointed out, "but I wound up driving away the best thing that ever happened to me and I'll do anything to get her back."

"Oh Everett," Schuyler said, emotion in her tone, "that is deeply, deeply romantic—and deeply, deeply flawed. You're going to wind up failing and having your heart broken into a thousand little pieces, and then ground up into dust after that."

"I don't want to hear about it, Schuyler," he told his sister with finality. "I don't need you to tell me how I can fail. I need you to tell me that I'll get her back. I *need* to get her back," he emphasized.

He heard Schuyler sigh, as if she was surrendering. "Okay. Just please, *please* don't do anything stupid," his sister warned.

"I already did," Everett told her. "I let Lila go in the first place."

"Everett—"

"I'll be in touch, Schuy," he told her before he terminated the call.

Everett gave it to the count of ten, then opened his phone again. He had a call to make and then he had to get back on the road if he wanted to reach Houston before nightfall.

Lila didn't need to get back to the office that quickly. She'd just told Everett that she did so she had a way to end their lunch. She'd estimated that half an hour in his company was about all she could take.

She had a feeling that if she came back early, the people she worked with, the ones who seemed to take such an inordinate interest in her life, would be all over her with questions.

Especially Lucie.

But if she timed it just right, she could slip into the office just as they were coming back from their own lunches. That way she stood a better chance of avoiding any questions.

She thought it was a good plan and it might have actually worked—if it hadn't been for the flowers. Two dozen long stemmed red roses in a glass vase to be precise. They were right there, in the middle of her desk, waiting for her when she walked into the office an hour after she'd left.

And there, right next to the vase, was Lucie. With a broad smile on her face.

"You just missed the delivery guy," she told Lila. "I signed for them for you."

"Um, thank you," Lila murmured, although what she was really thinking was that Lucie shouldn't have bothered doing that.

"No problem," Lucie answered cheerfully. Her eyes were practically sparkling as she looked from the flowers to her friend. It was obvious that she had barely been able to curtail her curiosity and keep from reading the card that had come with the roses. "Who are they from?"

"I have no idea," Lila murmured, eyeing the roses uneasily, as if she expected them to come to life and start taunting her.

"You know a really good way to find out?" Lucie asked her innocently. When Lila glanced in her direction, Lucie told her with great clarity: "Read the card."

Lila nearly bit off that she *knew* that. Instead, resigned, she said, "I guess I'll have to."

"Boy, if someone sent me roses, I'd sound a lot happier than that," Lucie commented.

"Want them?" Lila offered, ready to pick up the vase and hand it over to her friend.

"I'd love them," Lucie said with feeling. "But I can't take them. They're yours. Now who sent them?" Her eyes narrowed as she looked directly into Lila's.

Steeling herself, Lila reached over and plucked the small envelope stuck inside the roses. Slowly opening it, she took out the off-white rectangular card.

Till next time. Everett.

Her hand closed around the card. She was tempted to crush the small missive, but something held her back.

Damn it, why couldn't the man take a hint? Why was he determined to haunt her life this way? Why couldn't he just stay away the way he had done for the last thirteen years?

"Well?" Lucie asked, waiting. She tried to look over her friend's shoulder to read the card. "Who sent the flowers?"

"Nobody," Lila answered evasively.

"Well 'nobody' must have some pretty deep pockets," Lucie commented, eyeing the roses. "Do you know what roses are going for these days?"

"I don't know and I don't care," Lila answered defiantly. She was debating throwing the card into the trash.

"Well, 'nobody' certainly does. Care, I mean," Lucie clarified. "By any chance, are these flowers from the guy you went out to lunch with?"

Lila closed her eyes. She really did wish she could convincingly carry off a lie, but she couldn't. Absolutely no answer came to her, so she found herself having to admit the truth.

"Maybe."

Lucie gave a low whistle as she regarded the roses. "All I can say is that you must have made one hell of an impression at lunch."

"No, I didn't," Lila replied. "He asked if he

could call me again and I told him I didn't think that was such a good idea."

Taking in the information, Lucie nodded. "Playing hard to get. That really turns some guys on," she confided. "They see it as a challenge."

"I'm not playing hard to get," Lila stressed between gritted teeth. "I'm playing impossible to get."

"Same thing for some guys," Lucie responded knowingly. "What you did was just upped the ante without realizing it. Play out the line a little bit, then tell him that you've had a change of heart because he's so persistent. Then reel him in."

She felt like her back was up against the wall and Lucie was giving her fishing analogies. She looked at the other woman in disbelief. "You're telling me I should go out with him?"

"What I'm telling you is that you should give him another chance," Lucie told her.

Another chance. She knew that was what Everett wanted as well, even though he'd started out by acting as if he didn't, Lila thought. But there was no other reason why he would want to call her the next time he was in Austin *unless* he wanted another chance. It certainly wasn't because they'd had such a spectacular time today at lunch and he wanted to continue that.

They hadn't been spectacular together in a long, long time, Lila thought.

She tried to close her mind off from the memories, but they insisted on pushing their way through, punching through the fabric of the years.

Echoes from the past both softened her and squeezed her heart, reminding her of the pain she'd gone through at the end.

How could she willingly open herself up to that again? She'd barely recovered the last time.

Lila blinked. Lucie was standing in front of her, waving her hand in front of her eyes.

"Hey, Earth to Lila. Earth to Lila," Lucie called out.

"What?" Lila responded, stopping short of biting off an angry cry.

"I was talking to you and you seemed like you were a million miles away. Where were you just now?"

Lila blew out a quick breath and pulled herself together.

"You called it," she told the other woman. "I

was a million miles away. And now it's time to come back and get to work," she announced. "I've got a stack of reports to review so I can make the rounds tomorrow."

Lucie inclined her head. "I can take a hint."

"I certainly hope so," Lila murmured under her breath.

Hearing her, Lucie added, "For now," as she left the room.

Lila suppressed a groan. Glaring at the roses, she moved the vase to the windowsill.

It didn't help.

CHAPTER FIVE

"HAVE YOU GIVEN 'Mr. Roses' any more thought?" Lucie asked her a few days later completely out of the blue.

They were each preparing their input to submit for their departments' monthly budget and, taking a break, Lucie had peered into her office to ask about Everett.

Surprised by the unexpected salvo—she'd thought she was out of the woods since Lucie hadn't brought the subject up for several days—Lila answered, "None whatsoever." She deliberately avoided Lucie's eyes as she said it.

"You're lying," Lucie said.

This time Lila did look up. She shot her a look that was just short of a glare, but Lucie wasn't intimidated.

"You know how I know?" Lucie asked her.

Lila braced herself inwardly. Her outward

countenance didn't change. "Please, enlighten me," she requested coolly.

"You're blushing," Lila pointed out triumphantly. "Every time you say something that you're not entirely comfortable about—like a little white lie—you start to blush."

Lila drew herself up. "I do not," she protested. But even as she said it, she could feel her cheeks getting warmer.

"Got a mirror?" Lucie asked. She appeared to be serious. "I'll show you."

Lila sighed, dropping her head back. "Okay, so I've thought about him, but the answer to your next question is still 'no.' I'm not going to be seeing him again anytime soon—*or ever.*"

Lucie shook her head. It was obvious by her expression that she thought Lila was turning her back on a golden opportunity.

"I think you're making a mistake," Lucie told her in no uncertain terms.

"My mistake to make," Lila informed her cheerfully. And then, because she knew that Lucie was only looking out for her, she relented. "No offense, Lucie. I know you're a romantic at heart. I'm aware of your story," she went on.

"You and Chase were teenage sweethearts who, despite a few bumps on the road—"

"Big bumps," Lucie emphasized, interjecting her own narrative.

"—were meant to be together," Lila continued, pushing on. "But not everyone is like you. Most teenage sweethearts usually outgrow each other and are meant to be apart."

"Aha," Lucie exclaimed. "So you two were teenage sweethearts."

Lila stared at her. That had been a slip. "I didn't say that," she protested.

"Not in so many words," Lucie countered. "But you definitely implied it. Lila," she said, lowering her voice as she put her hand over her friend's. "The heart wants what the heart wants and it doesn't always make perfect sense. But old loves imprint themselves on your heart and on your brain. Take it from me. They *always* stay with you."

"That might have been your experience," Lila granted. "And I know that you and Chase are extremely happy—"

"We are," Lucie assured her.

Lila forged on. "—but not everyone is like

you," she concluded. "As a matter of fact, I'm pretty sure that very few people are like you."

Apparently her remark didn't satisfy Lucie, who went on. "Why don't you give this guy another chance and see if you belong to the 'very few?'" she suggested.

Lila went back to looking over her notes and figures for the budget. "Not going to happen."

Lila might have wanted to drop the subject, but Lucie obviously didn't. The subject of reunited lovers was something that was near and dear to her heart.

"Why?" Lucie asked her. "What are you so afraid of, Lila?"

Lila's eyes met her friend's. "I'm afraid of not getting my budget done in time," she said in a crisp voice.

"Seriously," Lucie coaxed.

"Seriously," Lila insisted, refusing to be distracted from the subject any further.

Just then, she saw a movement out of the corner of her eye. She looked toward the doorway. For a split second, she was afraid that Everett had found his way up to the office, but then she realized, as the man drew closer, that it was

a deliveryman—and he was carrying another
vase filled with flowers.

Not again!

"Oh, look, more roses," Lucie announced
gleefully. "Just in time to replace the ones that
are beginning to wilt," she added, grinning at
Lila.

"How do you know they're for me?" Lila
asked almost defensively. "There are plenty of
other people who work here."

"Oh, I just have a feeling," Lucie told her, her
eyes sparkling as she looked at her.

Her grin grew wider as the deliveryman came
over to Lila's office where they were working.

"Ms. Clark?" the deliveryman asked, looking
from one young woman to the other.

"That would be her," Lucie said, pointing toward Lila.

With a nod of his head, the deliveryman
offered Lila what looked like a rectangular,
brown Etch A Sketch.

"Would you sign here for the flowers, please?"
the man requested.

Though she was strongly tempted to refuse

the flowers, Lila didn't want to create problems for the deliveryman, so she did as he had said.

Then he indicated the flowers. "Where do you want them?" he asked her.

"Be nice, Lila," Lucie cautioned, as if she could see that her friend was tempted to tell the man exactly where she wanted him to put the roses.

Resigned, Lila told the deliveryman, "I'll take them."

When she did, she realized that this vase felt even heavier than the last one had. Looking closer, she saw that the vase appeared to be cut crystal.

"Have a nice day," the deliveryman told her cheerfully, retreating.

"With those roses, how could she do otherwise?" Lucie asked, calling after him.

"You like them so much, here, you take them," Lila said, trying to hand the vase over to the other woman.

But Lucie raised her hands up high, putting them out of reach and thus keeping the transfer from being carried out.

"You know what this means, don't you?" she asked Lila.

"That the price of roses is being driven up even higher?" Lila asked sarcastically.

Lucie shook her head. She looked very pleased with this turn of events.

"No. It means that you might think you're done with this guy from your past, but he clearly is *not* done with you."

Lila had another take on the situation. "Maybe he's just not used to taking no for an answer," she countered, frowning, then insisted, "All these flowers don't mean anything."

"You know, you still haven't answered my question," Lucie said, watching as Lila placed the flowers on the windowsill beside the other vase.

Lila didn't bother fussing with the newest arrangement. Instead, she sat down at her desk again, still trying to focus on the budget that was due. "What question is that?"

Slowly, enunciating each word for emphasis, Lucie repeated, "What are you afraid of?"

"I thought I answered that," Lila told her. "I believe I said I was afraid of not getting my budget done in time."

Lucie's eyes met hers. "You know I'm just going to keep after you until you tell me what's up with you and this guy."

And she knew very well that Lucie would, Lila thought. This had to stop. It was bad enough she was trying to get Everett to back off and leave her alone. She did *not* need her friend championing Everett's cause as well.

"Lucie, I love you like a sister—but butt out," she told Lucie in no uncertain terms.

"Sorry," Lucie replied, looking at her innocently. "That doesn't compute."

Lila rolled her eyes. "*Make* it compute," she told Lucie and with that, she ushered the woman out and closed the door to her office because, all distractions and two dozen roses aside, she really *did* have a budget to hand in before the end of the week. Which meant that she had no time to think about Everett Fortunado and his attempts to get her to give him another chance to shatter her heart.

The roses on the windowsill were beginning to drop their petals. They fell sporadically, drifting like soft pink tears onto the industrial beige floor covering in her office.

There was something sad about watching the flowers wilt.

Or maybe she felt that way because, despite the two separate deliveries of long-stem roses, she had not heard from Everett since she'd left him in the restaurant on their one and only lunch date—if it could actually have been called that.

Lila told herself that she was relieved. If Everett didn't call, then she didn't have to come up with an excuse not to see him.

But amid all that so-called relief, she had to admit that there was just the slightest tinge of disappointment as well. She really hadn't thought that Everett would give up so easily, or so quickly.

But he obviously had.

He'd moved on and he was off her conscience—not that she'd ever done anything to feel guilty about when it came to Everett, she silently insisted. Everett, on the other hand, had a lot to atone for—

What was wrong with her? she suddenly

upbraided herself. Why was she wasting time thinking about Everett or trying to figure out why he'd behaved the way he had? She didn't have time for all that, she admonished herself. Less time than usual.

She was in the middle of a very real health crisis.

Everyone at the Fortune Foundation was. They had been stricken by an unseasonable, full-fledged flu epidemic that was laying everyone low. As a result, they were understaffed, with almost a third of both the volunteers and employees alike calling in sick.

Being short-staffed when it came to the workers was one thing. But now two of the doctors who regularly volunteered their services, making the rounds and tending to the people in her district, had fallen sick and were out of commission as well.

What that meant in the short run was that there weren't enough doctors to administer the flu vaccines or to treat the people who were down with it.

This directly affected Lila, who oversaw the department that made certain poor families in her area had access to flu shots and to medical care.

She needed replacement for the sick doctors. STAT.

Lila had spent half the morning on the phones, calling every backup physician she could think of in the area. All the calls yielded the same results. The doctors were either up to their ears in patients—or they were sick themselves.

The cupboard, Lila thought, exasperated, was appallingly bare. There weren't any doctors in or around Austin left to call.

Frustrated, she closed her physicians' file on the computer. The people whose trust she had painstakingly worked to gain and whom she had gathered into the fold now needed help, and they were counting on her to come through. They weren't going to believe her when she said that she couldn't find any doctors to make house calls.

But it was true. She was totally out of doctors to call. Totally out of options…

Except for one, she suddenly realized as the thought zigzagged through her brain.

She hated to do this. Hated to have to call him and sound as if she was begging.

But this wasn't about her, Lila reminded herself. This was about the sick people who were counting on her. People who were in desperate need of medical care. Otherwise, some of them, the very young and the very old, might not make it.

Telling herself not to think about what she was doing, Lila took out the card Everett had handed her during the less than successful lunch. The card with his phone number on it.

Not his cell phone. She didn't want this to sound personal, although *that*, she had a feeling, might get the fastest results.

Lila squared her shoulders and rejected the thought about using Everett's cell phone number. She was going to try his office phone number first—and pray that she got through that way.

Tapping out the number on her landline, Lila found herself connected to a recording with a list of menu options.

Feeling unusually short-tempered, Lila nearly hung up at that point. But she forced herself to stay on. This was about the kids, she reminded herself. The kids, not her. She needed to try every available possibility.

After dutifully listening to the selections, she pressed "Number 4 for Dr. Fortunado."

That connected her to yet another recording, which asked her to leave her name, phone number and a brief message. The recording promised her a return call within twenty-four hours. It didn't sound reassuring, but she supposed that it was better than nothing.

The second the "beep" went off, Lila began talking.

"Everett, it's Lila. I'm sorry to bother you like this, but we've been hit really hard with this flu epidemic. I'm down two doctors, not to mention a number of staff members. Every backup physician I've called is already handling too many patients—if they're not sick themselves. I'm totally out of options, otherwise I wouldn't be bothering you. I know you're an internist and not a family practitioner, but to put it quite simply, I'm desperate. A lot of the people I interact with are down with this flu and I need help.

"If you're too busy to return this call, I'll understand. However, I hope you'll consider it. You can reach me in my office, or on my cell." She proceeded to recite both numbers slowly. "I hope to hear from you soon, but like I said, if you decide you can't help, I'll understand."

With that, she hung up and desperately tried to think of some other course of action. Maybe she could try physicians' assistants in the area. The way she saw it, it was any port in a storm at this point.

But she just ran into wall after wall.

Lila was beginning to think that the situation was hopeless.

And then her phone rang.

Snatching the receiver up, she cried, "This is Lila Clark," as she literally crossed her fingers, hoping that one of the many, *many* doctors she had called today was calling back to tell her that after due consideration, they had found a way to spare a few hours to work with the needy families.

"Lila," the deep voice on the other end of the line said. "It's Everett."

CHAPTER SIX

As the sound of his voice registered, Lila felt as if everything had suddenly ground to a standstill all around her.

But maybe her imagination was playing tricks on her, or she had just heard incorrectly and *thought* it was Everett calling her. Someone else might have said that wishful thinking was to blame, but she refused to call it that.

Rousing herself, Lila asked in a small, stilted voice, "Everett?"

"Yes."

She exhaled a shaky breath before saying his name, as if to make certain that it really was him calling. "Everett."

Had he gotten her message? Lila wondered. Or was this just a coincidence and he was calling because she hadn't acknowledged the roses he'd sent her? Taking nothing for granted, Lila replied, "I called you earlier today—"

"Yes, I know," he responded. "About a flu epidemic you're having in Austin. That's the reason I'm calling back. If you still need me, I can be there by tomorrow morning."

Relief swept over her, drenching her like a huge tidal wave and stealing her breath. Lila was certain she now understood how lottery winners felt.

"Oh, I need you," she said with feeling, and then she realized how that must have sounded to him. Mortified, Lila immediately backtracked. "That is... I mean—"

She heard Everett laugh softly. That same old laugh that used to make her skin tingle and had warm thoughts flowing all through her, fast and heavy.

"That's okay, I know what you meant," Everett assured her. "Are you really that short-handed out there?"

Looking at the mounting stack of calls on her desk, almost all requesting help, she stifled a groan. "You have no idea."

"Well, you can give me a tour and let me see what you're up against when I get there tomorrow," he told her.

She knew that Everett had his own practice and that he was going to have to make arrangements on his end in order to accommodate her, even for one day. It didn't take a genius to know that that he was really going out of his way for her.

"I can't begin to tell you how much I appreciate this, Everett," Lila began.

Everett cut her short. "I'm a doctor," he replied simply. "This is what I do." She heard papers being moved around on his end. "I should be able to get in by eight. Where should I meet you?"

This was really happening, she thought. Everett was actually coming to her rescue, despite the way everything had ended between them the last time they saw one another. Relief and gratitude mingled with a sharp twinge of guilt within her.

"Why don't we meet at the Fortune Foundation?" she suggested to him. "And we can go from there."

Lila went on to give him the address of the building, although that would have been easy enough for him to look up if he wanted to. She told him which floor she was on as well as the number of her office.

"I can wait outside the building for you if that'll be easier," Lila added.

"That won't be necessary," Everett assured her. "They taught me how to count in medical school."

Had she just insulted him somehow? Afraid of saying something wrong, Lila felt as if she was stumbling over her own tongue. "Oh, I'm sorry. I didn't mean to—"

"Lila," Everett raised his voice as he cut into her words. When she abruptly stopped talking, he told her, "Stop apologizing."

She took a deep breath, trying to center herself and regroup. None of this was easy for her. Not when it came to Everett. "Um, I guess I'm just not used to asking for favors."

Everett read between the lines. "Don't worry. I'm not going to ask you for a favor back if that's what you're thinking," he assured her. There was another moment of awkward silence on her end and then he said, "All right, if I'm going to be there tomorrow morning, I've got a few things to see about between now and then. See you tomorrow," he told her.

Everett hung up before she had a chance to thank him again.

Lila slowly returned the receiver back to its cradle. "Well," she murmured, still feeling somewhat numb as she continued to look at the receiver, "that at least solves some of my problem."

She was still one doctor down, but one out of two was a lot better in her opinion than none out of two, she told herself. She could definitely work with one.

In the meanwhile, she needed to get the list of patients prepared for the doctors who *were* coming in so that they could start making those house calls.

Lila looked down at the various names and addresses she'd already jotted down. The number of people who were just too ill to get to a local clinic on their own was astounding, and growing rapidly. Some of the people, she thought, were probably exaggerating their conditions, but she couldn't really blame them. The free clinics were always positively jammed from the moment they opened their doors in the morning. Waiting to be seen by a doctor was exceedingly challenging when you weren't running a fever. Sitting there with a fever of a hundred or more and feeling too weak to win a wrestling match against a flea was a whole different story. If she were in that position, she'd ask to have the doctor come to the house, too.

Oh, who are you kidding? You could be at death's door and you'd drag yourself in to see the doctor because you wouldn't want to inconvenience anyone.

Lila smiled to herself as she gathered her things together to meet with the physicians who were volunteering their time today.

The silent assessment rang true. She'd rather die than to surrender to her own weakness, Lila thought, going out the door.

Lila was exhausted.

Having stayed late, reorganizing supplies and hustling all over the city to beg, borrow or threaten to steal more vaccine serum as well as arranging for more lab tests to be done, she had finally dragged herself home after midnight.

Too tired to eat, she still hadn't been able to get right to sleep—most likely because part of her kept thinking about having to interact with Everett after she had summarily rejected him the last time they had been together.

But she had finally dropped off to sleep somewhere around 1:00 a.m., only to wake up at 4:30 a.m., half an hour before her alarm was set to go off.

She lay there for several minutes, staring at the ceiling, telling herself that she had half an hour before she needed to get up, which meant that she could grab a few more minutes of sleep.

She gave up after a couple more minutes, feeling that there was no point in trying to get back to sleep. She was wired and that meant she was up for the day.

With a sigh, she got up, showered and dressed. A piece of toast accompanied her to her car, along with a cup of coffee that would have been rejected by everyone except a person who felt they had no extra time to make a second, better cup of coffee.

Sticking the thick-sludge-contained-in-a-cup into a cup holder, Lila started the car.

There had to be a better way to achieve saint-hood, she thought cryptically to herself as she drove to the Foundation in the dark.

The streets were fairly empty at that time in the morning. The lack of light just intensified the pervasive loneliness that seemed to be invading every space in her head.

Snap out of it, damn it, she ordered. *He's a doctor and you need a doctor in order to help out. And that's all you need.*

However, ambivalent feelings about seeing Everett again refused to leave her alone. They continued to ricochet through her with an intensity that was almost numbing.

He's not Everett, she silently insisted. *He's just an available doctor who's willing to help you. That's what you have to focus on, not anything else, understand? Don't you dare focus on anything else.* She all but threatened herself.

It helped.

A little.

Arriving in the parking lot located behind the Fortune Foundation building, she found that there were only a few vehicles that pockmarked the area at this hour. Apparently the Foundation had a few early birds who liked to come in and get a jumpstart on the day and the work they had to do.

As she made her way toward the entrance, she saw that one of the cars, a navy blue high-end sedan, had someone sitting inside it in the driver's seat.

As she passed the vehicle, the driver's side door opened and Everett stepped out. A very casual-looking Everett wearing boots, jeans and a zippered sweatshirt with a hood.

She almost hadn't recognized him.

Her heart suddenly began to hammer very hard when she did.

"I got here early," he told her, nodding at Lila by way of a greeting. "Traffic from Houston wasn't too bad this time," he explained. He saw the way she was looking at what he was wearing. He looked down at his attire himself, just to be sure that he hadn't put anything on inside out. "I didn't want to look intimidating," he explained. "Someone told me that three-piece suits make some people nervous."

The way he said it, she felt as if he was implying she was the nervous person.

You've got to stop reading into things, she up-braided herself. Out loud she told him, "You look fine. We need to go in," she said, changing the subject as she turned toward the building. "I need to get a few things before we head out."

Everett nodded, gesturing toward the main doors. "You're the boss," he told her.

That almost made her wince. "This'll work better if you just think of me as your tour guide," she said, avoiding looking at him.

Holding the door open for her, Everett followed her into the building. "You told me that you manage the department," he recalled.

"I do," she answered cautiously, wondering where he was going with this.

"Then that would make you my boss for this," Everett concluded. "At least for now."

This had all the signs of degenerating into a dispute. But Everett *was* doing her a favor by coming in today and he was getting no compensation for it. She didn't want to pay him back by arguing with him.

"Whatever works for you is fine with me," Lila told him loftily.

He smiled at her as they headed toward the elevators. "I'll keep that in mind."

Was he just being agreeable, or was that some sort of a veiled warning, she wondered. This was all very exhausting and they hadn't even gotten started, Lila thought.

The next moment, as she got into the elevator, Lila told herself that any way she looked at it, this was going to be one hell of a long day.

But then, she had her doubts that Everett was going to be able to keep up. Making house calls to all the people on her list was going to turn into a marathon as well as an endurance test, at least for Everett.

And maybe her, too.

Getting what she needed from her office, Lila led the way back out of the building. "We'll use my car," she told him.

"Fair enough," Everett answered agreeably. "You know your way around here a lot better than I do."

"At least in the poor sections," she answered. They had barely gotten out on the road when she said, "Be sure to let me know when you've had enough."

He thought that was rather an odd thing to say, seeing as how they hadn't even been to see one patient yet. "And then what?" he wanted to know.

She spared him a glance as she drove through a green light. The answer, she thought, was rather obvious. "And then we'll stop."

"For the day?" he questioned.

"Well, yes." What else did he think she meant? They weren't talking about taking breaks.

"You made it sound like you needed me for the long haul," he said. And to him, that meant the entire day—with the possibility of more after that.

"I do." However, she didn't want to seem presumptuous and she definitely didn't want to totally wear him out. "But—"

"Well, then that's what you've got me for," Everett said, interrupting. "The long haul," he repeated.

Was he saying that to impress her, or did he really mean it, she wondered.

"I just wanted to warn you," she said as they drove to a run-down neighborhood. "This isn't going to be what you're used to."

He looked at her then. "No offense, Lila, but we haven't seen each other for a very long time," he reminded her. "You have no idea what I'm used to."

Everett was right, she thought, chagrined. She had no idea what he been doing in the years since they had seen one another. She knew, obviously, that he had achieved his dream and become a doctor. She had just assumed that he had set up a practice where he tended to the needs of the richer people in Houston. It never occurred to her that he might concern himself with even middle-class patients, much less those who belonged to the lower classes: the needy and the poor. And she had no idea that he ever volunteered his time to those less fortunate.

"You're right," she admitted quietly. "I don't. I just know that your parents had high hopes for you and that you weren't the rebellious type."

Everett was only half listening to her. For the most part, he was taking note of the area they were now driving through. It appeared seedy and dilapidated. It was light out now, which made the streets only a tad safer looking.

He tried to imagine what it was like, driving through here at night. "How often do you come out here?" he wanted to know.

"As often as I need to. I usually accompany the doctors who volunteer at the Foundation. It wouldn't be right to ask them to come here and not be their go-between."

"Go-between?"

She nodded. "Some of the doctors have never been to places like this before. They're uneasy, the patients they've come to treat are uneasy when they see the doctor. I'm kind of a human tranquilizer," she told him. "It's my job to keep them all calm and get them to trust each other enough so they can interact with one another," she explained.

"A human tranquilizer, huh?" he repeated with a grin, trying to envision that. "I kind of like that."

She laughed as she brought her small compact car to a stop in front of a ramshackle house that looked as if it was entering its second century.

"I had a feeling you would." Pulling up the hand brake, she turned off the ignition. "We're here," she announced needlessly. "You ready for this?" she asked, feeling somewhat uneasy for him.

Everett looked completely unfazed. "Let's do it," he told her, getting out on his side.

Lila climbed out on the driver's side, rounded the hood of her car and then led the way up a set of wooden stairs that creaked rather loudly with each step she took. Like the house, the stairs had seen better years and were desperately in need of repair.

Reaching the top step, she approached the front door with its peeling paint and knocked.

"The doorbell's out," she explained in case Everett was wondering why she hadn't rung it. "I've been here before," she added.

"That was my guess," Everett responded.

A moment later, the front door opened rather slowly. Instead of an adult standing on the other side, there was a small, wide-eyed little boy looking up at them. He was holding onto the doorknob with both hands.

In Everett's estimation, the boy couldn't have been any older than four.

CHAPTER SEVEN

LILA THOUGHT THAT Everett had dropped something when she saw him crouching down at the door of their first house call—single mother Mrs. Quinn. The next moment, she saw that what he was doing was trying to get down to the level of the little boy who stood across the threshold.

"Does your mom know you open the door to strangers?" Everett asked the boy.

The little boy shook his head from side to side, sending some of his baby-fine, soft blond hair moving back and forth about his face. "No. Mama's asleep next to my little brother."

"You're very articulate," Everett told the little boy. "How old are you?"

"Four," the boy answered, holding up four fingers so that there would be no mistaking what he said. "What's ar-tic—, ar-tic—" Giving up trying to pronounce the word, he approached it from another angle. "What you said," he asked, apparently untroubled by his inability to say the word.

"It means that you talk very well," Everett explained. Then he rose back to his feet. Glancing toward Lila so that the boy would know she was included, he requested, "Why don't you take us to see them? I'm a doctor," he added.

That seemed to do the trick. The little boy opened the door further, allowing them to come in. "Good, 'cause Mama said they need a doctor—her and Bobby," the four-year-old tacked on.

Impressed at how well Everett was interacting with the boy, Lila let him go on talking as she and Everett followed him through the cluttered house.

"Is Bobby your brother?" Everett asked.

This time the blond head bobbed up and down. "Uh-huh."

"And what's your name?" Everett asked, wanting to be able to address their precocious guide properly.

"Andy," the boy answered just as he reached the entrance to a minuscule bedroom. "We're here," he announced like the leader of an expedition at journey's end.

There was a thin, frail-looking dark-haired woman lying on top of the bed, her eyes closed, her arm wrapped around a little boy who was tucked inside the bed. The woman looked as if the years had been hard on her.

Andy tiptoed over to her and tried to wake her up by shaking her arm.

"Mama, people are here. Mama?" he repeated, peering into her face. He looked worried because her eyes weren't opening.

Lila finally spoke up. "Mrs. Quinn?" she said, addressing the boys' mother. "It's Lila. I brought a doctor with me."

The young woman's eyelashes fluttered as if she was trying to open them, but the effort was too much for her. She moaned something unintelligible in response to Lila's announcement.

Before Lila could say anything either to the woman or to Everett, he took over.

Moving Lila aside, he felt for the woman's pulse. Frowning, he went on to take her temperature next, placing a small, clear strip across her forehead.

"No thermometer?" Lila asked.

"This works just as well," he assured her. Looking at the strip, he nodded. "She's running a low-grade fever." Checking the boys' mother out quickly, he told Lila, "I can't give her a flu shot because she already seems to have it. But I can lower her fever with a strong shot of ac-etaminophen."

As Everett spoke, he took out a syringe and prepared it.

Andy's eyes followed his every move, grow-ing steadily wider. "Is my Mama gonna die?" he asked, fear throbbing in his voice.

"No, Andy. I'm going to make your mom all better. But you're going to have to be brave for all three of you," Everett told him. "Think you can do that?" he asked, talking to him the way he would to any adult.

The boy solemnly nodded his head. He held his breath as he watched his mother getting the injection.

"Good boy." Everett moved on to the wom-an's other son. "Looks like he's got it, too," he said to Lila. Turning to Andy, he asked him,

"Andy, do you know how long your mom and brother have been sick?"

Andy made a face as he tried to remember. He never took his eyes off the syringe, watching as the doctor gave his brother an injection next.

"Not long," Andy answered. "We were watching *Captain Jack* yesterday when Bobby said he didn't feel so good. Mama carried him to bed and she laid down, too."

Everett turned to look at Lila. *"Captain Jack?"* he questioned.

"It's a syndicated cartoon," Lila told him. "I think it airs around eight or so in the morning. One of the women in the office has a little boy who likes to watch it," she explained in case he wondered why she would know something like that.

"So Mrs. Quinn could have been sick for a couple of days?" Everett questioned, attempting to get a handle on how long mother and son had been down with the illness.

Lila was about to narrow it down a little more. "Mrs. Quinn called my office yesterday, but I didn't have anyone I could send."

Everett nodded, taking the information in. "You can only do as much as you can do," he told her. He knew Lila would beat herself up but it wasn't her fault. She couldn't make doctors appear out of thin air.

He performed a few tests on Mrs. Quinn and Bobby, and then he turned in Andy's direction. "It's your turn, Andy."

Andy looked totally leery as he slanted a long glance in the doctor's direction. "My turn for what?" he asked in a small voice.

"You get to be the one in your family to get a flu shot," Everett told him.

"But I don't want a shot. I'm not sick," Andy cried, his voice rising in panic.

"No, you're not," Everett agreed. "And if you let me give you a flu shot, you'll stay that way. Otherwise…" His voice trailed off dramatically.

Andy tried to enlist Lila to help him. She was just returning into the bedroom, bringing bottles of drinking water she'd brought with her in her car.

"But won't a flu shot give me the flu?" the boy asked, anticipatory tears of pain already gathering in his eyes.

"No, it acts like a soldier that keeps the flu away," Everett told him. "You don't want to get sick like your mom and your brother, do you?" Everett asked. "Someone's got to stay well to take care of them."

Andy looked torn, and then he sighed. "I guess you're right."

"Good man," Everett congratulated the little boy with hearty approval.

Lila set down the bottles of water as well as several pudding cups and bananas she'd brought in. "Attaboy," she said to Andy. "If you like, I'll hold you on my lap while Dr. Everett gives you that shot."

She didn't wait for the boy to answer. She gathered him up in her arms and held him on her lap.

"Okay, Dr. Everett. Andy's ready." She felt the little boy dig his fingers into her arm as Everett gave him the flu injection. She heard Andy breathe in sharply. "You were very brave," she commended the boy.

"I'll say," Everett said, adding his voice to praise the boy. As he packed up his bag, he looked around, concerned. "Is there anyone who can stay with the kids until Mrs. Quinn is well enough to take care of them?" he asked Lila in a low voice. "I don't like the idea of just leaving them this way."

"Mrs. Rooney comes by to stay with us some-times whenever Mama has to go out," Andy said, looking from the doctor to Lila as if to see if they thought that was good enough.

"Do you know where Mrs. Rooney lives?" Everett asked Lila.

"I think that's the woman next door," she told him before Andy could respond. Shifting Andy off her lap, she rose to her feet. "I can go and knock on her door," she volunteered.

"We'll go together," Everett told her. When she looked at him quizzically, he said, "You shouldn't be out there alone."

In a low voice, she told Everett, "I've been dealing with people in this neighborhood and places *like* this neighborhood for several years now. You don't have to worry about me."

"No," Everett agreed. "I don't 'have to.' But since I'm here, I'd feel better going with you," he told her, adding, "Humor me."

Instead of answering him, she looked at

Andy, who was rubbing his arm where he had received his vaccination. "Andy, do you know if Mrs. Rooney does live next door?" she asked.

Sniffing as he blinked to keep big tears from falling, Andy nodded. "Uh-huh, she does."

Lila smiled at Everett. "Problem solved. I'll just pop in next door and ask the woman to keep an eye on this family."

She glanced at her watch. They had spent more time here than she'd anticipated. She was glad that it had gone so well for Everett, but they did need to speed things up.

"And then we're going to have to get a move on," she told Everett. "Otherwise, we're not going to get to see all the people on my list unless we work through the night and possibly into the next morning."

He hadn't thought that there were going to be *that* many houses to visit. But as far as he knew, Lila had never been one to exaggerate.

"Then you'd better find out if Mrs. Rooney is willing to stay with Andy and his family," he urged.

That went off without a hitch.

After getting the woman to stay with the

Quinn family, Lila drove herself and Everett to the second name on her list.

Again she was treated to observing Everett's bedside manner. She was completely amazed by how easily he seemed to get along with children. Not only get along with them but get them to trust him and rather quickly.

She smiled to herself as she recalled worrying that he might frighten the children because he'd be too stiff or too cold with them, but that definitely didn't turn out to be the case. Right from the very beginning, she saw that Everett knew exactly how to talk to the children.

Moreover, he acted as if he actually *belonged* in this sort of a setting.

Talk about being surprised, she mused.

As they drove from one house to another, Lila found herself wondering what these people who had so little would think if they knew that the man who was administering their vaccinations, writing out their prescriptions and listening so intently to them as they described their symptoms was actually a millionaire's son with a thriving, fancy practice back in Houston.

She laughed quietly to herself. They'd probably think that she was making it up because Everett seemed so down-to-earth, not to mention so focused on making them feel better.

As she continued observing Everett in setting after setting, Lila could feel her heart growing softer and softer.

It became harder for her to regard Everett in any sort of a cold light and practically impossible for her to keep the good memories at bay any longer.

Everett had grown into the good, decent man she had, in her heart, always felt that he was destined to become.

"How many more?" Everett asked her as they drove away from yet another house.

He and Lila had been at it for a straight twelve hours, stopping only to pick up a couple of hamburgers to go at a drive-through. They ate the burgers while driving from one patient to the next.

Keeping her eyes on the road as she drove, Lila smiled at his question. She didn't have to pull out her list to answer him. "That was the last house on my list."

"No more left?" Everett questioned, thinking that she might have accidentally overlooked one or two more patients.

"Nope, no more left," Lila told him. She flashed him a relieved grin to underscore her words.

"Wow." Everett leaned his head back against his headrest. "I was beginning to feel like we were going to go on with these house calls forever."

She laughed. "Does feel that way, doesn't it?" She spared him a glance as she came to a stop at a light. "Bet you're sorry now that you returned my call yesterday."

"No," Everett responded quite seriously. "I'm not."

After twelve hours of work on very little sleep, all she should be thinking about was getting some rest, nothing else. So why in heaven's name did she suddenly feel what amounted to an all-consuming hot tingle passing over the length of her body just because Everett had said that he wasn't sorry he'd called her back?

What was wrong with her?

Punchy, she was punchy. That had to be it, Lila decided.

Talk, damn it. Say something! she ordered herself. The silence was getting deafening.

Clearing her throat, Lila said, "Well, I have to admit that you surprised me today."

"Oh?" Everett responded. "How so?"

Lila was honest with him. She felt it was the best way. "I didn't think you had it in you to just keep going like this. And I really didn't think you knew how to talk to children."

"Why?" he asked. "Children are just short adults."

Lila laughed, shaking her head. "You would be surprised how many doctors don't really know how to talk to fully grown adults, much less to little children," she told him.

"That's right," Everett recalled. "When we started out today you told me that you were there to act as the go-between." He continued to look at her profile, curious. "So I guess I passed the test?"

The light turned green and Lila pressed down on the accelerator. Once they were moving again, she answered, "With flying colors." Again she felt she had to tell him how surprised she was by his performance. "I didn't think that you'd keep at it long enough to see all the people on the list." She struggled to stifle a yawn. The long day was catching up to her. "But it's kind of late now," she told him needlessly.

"It is," he agreed.

She glanced at the clock on the dashboard, even though she already knew what time it was. "Too late for you to be driving back to Houston tonight," she told him.

"Are you offering to put me up?" he asked, doing his best to keep a straight face.

That startled her. "What? No, I just—"

"Take it easy," he laughed. "You don't have to worry. I've already talked to Schuyler. She's expecting me. I'm spending the night at her place."

"So that means that you're not going back until sometime tomorrow?" Lila asked.

He laughed again. "I can see the wheels turning in your head. No, I'm not going back to Houston until the day after tomorrow. So, if you want me to make a few more house calls with you tomorrow, I'm available."

That would be a huge help. She was still

down a few volunteer doctors and she still hadn't found any more replacements.

"Don't toy with me, Everett," she told him, casting a glance his way.

His eyes were smiling at her. "I wouldn't dream of it."

Her heart fluttered. She forced herself to face forward. "All right. If you don't mind putting in some more time, then yes, absolutely. I could *really* use you for however much time you can spare."

"All right, then, same time tomorrow?" he asked as she pulled into the Foundation's parking lot.

"Make it eight-thirty," she told him.

"I'll be there," he promised, getting out of her car.

"If you decide to change your mind," she began, feeling obligated to give him a way out. After the day he had put in today, she didn't want to force him to come in tomorrow.

But Everett cut her off. "I won't," he told her just before he walked over to his own car.

Lila caught herself smiling. She knew he meant it.

CHAPTER EIGHT

WHEN LILA GOT up the next morning, she felt absolutely wiped out. If possible, she was even more tired than the day before. It was as if her get-up-and-go had physically gotten up and left.

"You're just burning the candle at both ends," she told the tired-looking reflection staring back at her in the bathroom mirror. "And maybe a little in the middle as well."

The shower did not invigorate her the way it usually did.

Dragging herself over to her closet after her shower, Lila pulled out the first things she found and got dressed. She was staring down the barrel of another grueling day, but at least she had a doctor for part of it, she thought. And after Everett left for Houston, maybe she would get lucky and be able to scrounge up another volunteer physician to conduct the house calls that were left on the list.

Determined to make herself look a little more human than what she saw in her mirror, Lila patiently applied her makeup. She succeeded in making herself look a little less exhausted—or at least less like someone who had recently been run over by a truck. The last thing she wanted was to have Everett take one look at her this morning and breathe a sigh of relief that he had dodged a bullet thirteen years ago.

Lila was still struggling to pull herself out of what was for her an atypical funk when she drove to the Foundation. This just wasn't like her, she thought. No matter how tired she felt, she never dragged like this, as if there was lead in her limbs.

C'mon, snap out of it! she silently ordered.

Just like the day before, when she drove into the parking lot, she found Everett sitting in his car, waiting for her.

When Everett saw her car approaching, he quickly got out of his vehicle. The cheery greeting on his lips didn't get a chance to materialize because he took a closer look at her as she got out of her car.

"Are you feeling all right, Lila?" he asked her.

So much for makeup saving the day, Lila thought. "I'm just running a little behind," she answered, deliberately being vague. Changing the subject, she asked, "Do I have you for half a day—or less?"

Rather than give Lila a direct answer, Everett told her, "Why don't we play it by ear and see?"

Lila put her own spin on his words. Everett was setting the stage so he could bail whenever he felt as if he'd had enough. Not that she blamed him, she thought. The man had already given a hundred and fifty percent of his time yesterday, far more than she had the right to expect, and she couldn't be greedy.

The hell she couldn't, Lila caught herself thinking. After all, this wasn't about her. This was about all those people who were counting on her to find a way to keep them healthy—or get them healthy—and at the very least, that involved having a doctor pay them a house call.

"Okay," Lila said with all the pseudo enthusiasm she could muster as she opened the passenger door for Everett. "Let's get started."

"How do you do this every day?" Everett wanted to know after they had made more than half a dozen house calls.

"Doctors used to do this all the time," she told Everett.

It took him a moment to understand what Lila was referring to. He realized that they weren't on the same page.

"I'm not talking about the house calls," Everett told her. "I'm talking about seeing this much poverty and still acting so cheerful when you talk to the people."

"I'm being cheerful *for* their sake. An upbeat attitude brings hope with it," she told him. "And hope and perseverance are practically the only way out of these neighborhoods," Lila maintained.

Everett was more than willing to concede the point. "You probably have something there." And then he blew out a breath, as if mentally bracing himself for round two. "How many more people are on that famous list of yours for today?" he wanted to know.

It was already closer to one than to noon. Did he know that, she wondered. They'd been at this for hours and she'd assumed that no matter what he'd said on the outset, she just had him for half a day.

"Don't you have a plane to catch or a car to drive?" she asked.

"Trying to get rid of me?" he asked her, an amused expression on his face.

"No, on the contrary, trying not to take you for granted and start relying on you too much," Lila corrected. And in a way, that was true. That had been her downfall all those years ago. She'd just expected to be able to rely on Everett forever. And look how that had turned out, she thought. Determined to pin him down, she asked, "How long did you say you could work today?"

"I didn't, remember?" he reminded her.

"Right. You said, quote, 'why don't we play it by ear and see,'" Lila recalled.

"Well, it still seems to be going, doesn't it?" he observed, his expression giving nothing away. "Who's next on the list?" he asked, redirecting her attention back to the immediate present.

Eyes on the road, Lila put one hand into the purse she kept butted up next to her and pulled out the list of patients that she'd put right on top. All she needed was a quick glance at the page.

"Joey Garcia's next," she answered. "Joey's the baby of the family," she added, giving Everett an encapsulated summary of his next patient. "He's got two big sisters and two big brothers and he always gets everything after the rest of the family's gotten over it.

"However, according to my records," she said, trying to recall what she had entered on her tablet, "I don't think anyone in the family has had the flu *or* gotten the vaccine this year."

"Well, I guess we're about to find out, aren't we?" Everett speculated as she pulled the car up before another house that looked as if it might have been new over fifty years ago.

Lila got out on her side and immediately found that she had to pause for a moment. She held onto the car door for support. Everything around her had suddenly opted to wobble just a little, making her head swim and the rest of her extremely unsteady.

Realizing that she wasn't with him as he approached the house, Everett looked back over his shoulder. "Something wrong?"

"No." Lila refused to tell him she'd felt dizzy, especially since the feeling had already passed. She didn't want to sound whiny or helpless and she definitely didn't want him fussing over her. "Just trying to remember if I forgot something."

Everett thought that sounded rather odd. What could she have forgotten? "Did you?"

"No," she answered rather abruptly. "I've got everything."

He played along for her sake. She didn't look as if she was herself today.

"I don't know how you manage to keep track of everything," he told her as they approached the Garcias' front door.

"It's a gift," Lila told him wryly. She forced a wide smile to her lips as she fervently wished that she'd stop feeling these odd little waves of weakness that kept sweeping over her.

Taking a deep breath, she knocked on the

front door. It swung open immediately. The next moment, she was introducing Everett to a big, burly man who appeared to be almost as wide as he was tall.

"Mr. Garcia, this is Dr. Everett Fortunado. He'll be giving you and your family your flu vaccinations," Lila told Juan Garcia and the diminutive wife standing next to him.

The couple went from regarding Everett suspiciously to guardedly welcoming him into their home.

"The children are in the living room," Mrs. Garcia said, leading the way through what amounted to almost railroad-style rooms to the back of the house.

As he walked into the living room, Everett was immediately aware of five pairs of eyes warily watching his every move.

Everett did his best to set the children at ease, talking to them first and asking their names. He explained exactly what he was about to do and what they could expect, including how the vaccine felt going into their arms.

When he was done, he surprised Lila by

handing out small candy bars to each child. "For being brave," he told them.

"That was nice of you," Lila said as they left the Garcias' house twenty minutes later.

Everett shrugged. "Candy makes everything better." He got into the car. "I thought you said they called you."

"Well, sometimes I call them," Lila replied. She could feel Everett regarding her quizzically as she pulled back onto the street. "Mr. Garcia is very proud. He doesn't like accepting help. He's also out of work. I thought he and his family could do with a little preventative medicine so that if a job *does* come up, he won't be too sick to take it. He's a day laborer when he's not driving a truck," she explained. When Everett didn't say anything, she elaborated on her statement. "The man has five kids. If they all came down with the flu, it would be guaranteed pure chaos. This was a pre-emptive strike."

That was one way to look at it, Everett thought. Obviously Lila was focused on doing good deeds. "So when did you get fitted for the wings and halo?" Everett asked her.

"I didn't," she answered crisply. "They were left behind by the last department manager." She kept her eyes on the road, not trusting herself to look at him. Sudden movements made her dizzy. "I just try them on for size occasionally."

"Oh." He pretended as if what she'd just said made perfect sense. "So, how many more house calls do we have left?" he asked, getting serious again.

This time Lila didn't have to consult her list. "We've got two more."

"Just two more?" he questioned. Yes, they'd been at this for a long time, but he'd just expected to keep going until almost nightfall again, the way they had yesterday.

"Just two more," Lila repeated. "And then you're free."

"Free, eh?" he echoed. He studied her profile. "How about you?"

"How about me what?" she asked. Had she missed a question? Her brain felt a little fuzzy and she was having trouble following him.

"Are you free?" Everett asked, enunciating each word clearly.

"Free for what?" she asked. She was still having trouble following him.

"Free for dinner," he asked, then quickly added, "I thought that maybe, since we've developed this decent working relationship, you wouldn't mind grabbing some dinner together."

Lila pressed her lips together. All she'd been thinking about the last few hours was going home and crawling into bed. But she was not about to tell Everett that. She didn't want to have to listen to a lot of questions.

So instead, sounding as cheerful as possible, she said, "I guess I do owe you that."

"I don't want you to have dinner with me because you 'owe' me," he told her. "I want you to have dinner with me because you want to."

Potato, po-tah-to, she thought. He'd come through for her, so she supposed that she could humor him. "I want to," she answered quietly.

"Great," he said. "Let's go see these last two patients."

The visits took a little longer than he'd come to anticipate, mainly because the second one involved more than just dispensing flu vaccinations to the two older children and their parents. Everett found himself tending to a pint-size patient with a sprained wrist that he didn't even know he had.

Afraid of being laughed at by his brothers for being clumsy, when it was his turn for the vaccine, little Alan had tried to hide his swollen wrist.

Drawing him over to Everett, Lila had accidentally brushed against the boy's wrist and saw him wince, then try to pretend he was just playing a game with her. The truth came out rather quickly.

"Never try to hide something like that," Lila told him as Everett bandaged the boy's wrist and then fashioned a makeshift sling for him. "They just get worse if you ignore them," she told him.

Alan solemnly nodded his head.

"He's been moping all day," Alan's mother told them as they were packing up their supplies. "Now I know why. Here," she said handing Lila a pie, which, by its aroma, had just recently left the oven. "This is my way of saying thank-you."

Lila declined. "As a Foundation worker, I can't accept payment," she told the other woman.

"Then take it as a friend," Alan's mother told her. "One friend to another. You will be insulting me if you don't accept it," the woman insisted.

The way she felt, Lila was not up to arguing. Pulling her lips back into a thin smile, she expressed her thanks, saying, "Dr. Everett will take it home with him. Maybe your gift will encourage him to return to Austin again soon."

The woman was obviously pleased to play her part in coaxing the good-looking doctor back.

"Maybe," she agreed, flashing a bright, hopeful smile at Everett.

"I wouldn't have thought of that," Everett told Lila when they were back in her car again. "That was quick thinking," he complimented her.

Lila was hardly aware of shrugging. "I didn't want to hurt her feelings, but I didn't want to set a precedent, either. Having you take it seemed like the only logical way out."

"Still wouldn't have thought of it," he told her.

"Sure you would have," she countered. "You're the smartest man I know."

No I'm not, he thought. He could cite a time when he'd been downright stupid.

Like thirteen years ago.

Everett studied her quietly as she drove. In his opinion, Lila had blossomed in the intervening years. She was no longer that stricken young girl who'd told him she never wanted to see him again. She'd become a self-assured woman who obviously had a mission in life. A mission she was passionate about, and that passion made her particularly compelling and exciting.

He found himself being attracted to Lila all over again and even more strongly this time than he had the first time around.

"Can you clock out once we get back to the Foundation?" he asked suddenly, breaking the heavy silence in the car.

"This actually is the official end of my day, so yes, I can clock out."

"And we're still on for dinner?" he asked, not wanting to come across as if he was taking anything for granted. He knew that winning Lila back was going to take time and patience—and he very much intended to win her back.

"If you still want to have dinner with me, then yes, we're still on," she answered cautiously. She made a right turn, pulling into the parking lot. "Are you sure this won't interfere with you getting back to Houston? I feel guilty about keeping you away from your practice for so long."

"Nothing to feel guilty about," he assured her. "The choice was mine. And my practice is part of a group. We all pitch in and cover for one another if something comes up."

"And this qualifies as 'something?'" she asked him, a touch of amusement entering her voice.

"Oh, most definitely 'something,'" Everett assured her.

My lord, she was flirting with him, Lila realized. She really wasn't herself.

The next moment, there was further proof. "Lila, you're passing my car," Everett pointed out.

Preoccupied and trying to get a grip on herself, she hadn't realized that she had driven right by the navy blue sedan.

"Sorry," she murmured. "Just double-check-
ing the schedule in my head."

"Schedule?" he questioned. But she'd said
there was no one left on today's list, didn't she?
Was there some secondary list he didn't know
about?

"The list of patients," she clarified.

"Did we miss anyone?" he asked, wondering
if she was going to find some excuse to turn
him down at the last minute.

She wished she didn't feel as if her brain had
a fog machine operating right inside her head.
It was getting harder and harder for her to think
straight.

"Lila?"

She realized that Everett was waiting for her
to answer him. "Oh, no, we didn't. We saw everyone on the list. I was just thinking about tomorrow," she lied. "Let's go have dinner."

"Sounds good to me," he replied, silently adding, *Anything that has to do with you sounds
good to me.*

CHAPTER NINE

"ON SECOND THOUGHT, maybe I should drive," Everett said to her just as Lila started her car up again.

Putting her foot on the brake now, Lila looked at Everett, confused.

"Why?" she wanted to know. "I know the city better than you do. You said so yourself."

"True, but I've been able to find my way around without much trouble and I don't mind driving. To be honest, you look like you're rather tired and you don't want to push yourself too hard," Everett stressed.

He was right. She *was* tired, Lila thought, but her pride kept her from admitting it. Her self-image dictated that she was supposed to be un-tiring, with boundless energy.

"Is that your professional opinion?" she asked.

"Professional and personal," Everett replied quietly.

There was that calming bedside manner of his again, Lila thought. But she wasn't a patient, she reminded herself.

"Tough to argue with that," she responded. "But you'll have to drive me back here after dinner so I can pick up my car."

Everett had already taken that into account. "No problem," he assured her. Getting out of her car, he took a few steps, then stood waiting for her to follow suit.

After a moment, Lila sighed, surrendering. Since she hadn't pulled out of the parking space yet, she left her car as it was and got out.

Crossing to his car, Everett unlocked it and then held the passenger side door open for her. After Lila got in, he closed the door and got in behind the wheel. He looked at her and smiled just before he started his car.

Was that smug satisfaction she saw, or something else? Lila wondered. "What?" she asked him.

"I thought you'd put up more of a fight," he confessed as he started up his vehicle. Within moments, they were on the road.

Lila lifted one shoulder in a careless shrug.

She realized that her shoulder felt heavy for some reason, like someone was pushing down on it. After dinner, she was heading straight for bed, she promised herself.

"I guess I'm more tired than I thought," she told Everett.

He accepted her excuse. "You in the mood for Chinese or Italian?" he asked, offering her a choice of the first two restaurants he thought of. He favored both.

"The Italian place is closer," Lila told him.

And in this case, he thought, closer seemed to mean better, otherwise she would have cited a different criterion first.

"Italian it is." He spared her one quick glance, coupled with a grin. "Now all you have to do is give me the address."

Lila dug in just for a second. "I thought you said you knew your way around."

"I do," he assured her, then added, "Once I have an address."

She laughed shortly. "That's cheating," Lila accused.

"I'd rather think of it as being creative," he told her, then asked again, "The address?"

She was much too tired to engage in any sort of a war of resistance. With a sigh, she rattled off the address to the Italian restaurant.

Everett immediately knew where it was. "You're right, that is close," he acknowledged.

They were there in less than ten minutes. As luck would have it, someone in the first row of the parking lot was just pulling out and Everett smoothly slipped right into the spot.

Shutting off his engine, he quickly came around to Lila's side.

Aware that Everett had opened the door for her, she felt a little woozy and it took her a moment to focus and swing her legs out. She really would have rathered that Everett wasn't holding the door open for her so he wouldn't see just how unsteady she was.

"You know, I have learned how to open my own door," she told him defensively.

If she was trying to antagonize him, Everett thought, he wasn't taking the bait.

"I know," he responded cheerfully. "I've seen you. But I like doing this," he told her, putting out his hand to her. "It makes me feel like a gentleman."

The wooziness retreated. Lila wrapped her fingers around his hand with confidence. Maybe she was worrying for no reason.

"Then I guess I'll humor you," she said, "seeing what an asset you were yesterday and today."

His smile sank deep into her very soul as he helped her out of the vehicle. "Whatever works."

Closing the door behind her, they crossed to the restaurant.

The homey, family-style restaurant was beginning to fill up, but there were still a number of empty tables available. The hostess seated them immediately and gave them menus.

"Do you come here often?" Everett asked Lila when they were alone.

"Often enough to know that they have good food," Lila answered.

Everett nodded. "Good, then I'll let you do the ordering," he told her, placing his menu on the table.

That surprised her. "Well, you certainly have changed," she couldn't help observing. When he raised an inquisitive eyebrow, she said,

"There was a time when you took charge of everything."

He couldn't very well argue the point. He remembered that all too well.

"I've learned to relax and take things light," he explained. "Somebody once told me I'd live a lot longer that way—or maybe it would just seem longer," he added with a laugh.

As their server approached the table Lila asked, "Were you serious about my doing the ordering for you?"

"Very."

Lila proceeded to order. "We'll have two servings of chicken Alfredo," she told the young woman. "And he'll have a side dish of stuffed mushrooms."

"And you?" the young woman asked, her finger hovering over her tablet.

"No mushrooms for me," Lila answered.

"And what would you like to drink?" the server asked, looking from Lila to the man she was sitting with.

"I'll have a glass of water," Lila answered, then looked at Everett, waiting for him to make a choice himself. She remembered he liked having wine with his meals, but maybe that had changed, too, along with his attitude.

"Make that two," Everett told the server, then handed over his unopened menu to her.

Lila surrendered hers after a beat.

"I'll be back with your bread and waters," the server told them.

"Sounds more like a prison diet than something from a homey-looking restaurant," Everett commented.

"That's probably what she thought, too," Lila said. "She looked like she was trying not to laugh." She looked around the large room. More patrons had come in moments after they did. "Certainly filled up fast," she observed, saying the words more to herself than to Everett.

"Worried about my being seen with you?" Everett asked, amused.

"No." She was actually thinking about how all those bodies were generating heat. "Does it seem rather warm in here to you?"

"Well, when you have this many bodies occupy a relatively small space, it's bound to feel somewhat warm," he speculated. And then he smiled. "You remembered I liked mushrooms," he said, clearly surprised.

"I remember a lot of things," she said, and then the next moment regretted it. "Like quadratic equations," she added glibly.

Everett laughed. And then he looked at her more closely. There was a line of perspiration on her forehead, seeping through her auburn bangs and pasting them to her forehead. "It's not warm enough in here to cause you to perspire," Everett observed.

"Maybe you make me nervous," Lila said flippantly.

"If that were the case, then you wouldn't have agreed to dinner," he pointed out. The woman he knew wouldn't do anything she didn't want to.

Lila shifted in her chair, growing progressively more uncomfortable. "It seemed impolite to turn you down after you went out of your way to be my white knight."

Her terminology intrigued him. "Is that what I am? Your white knight?" he asked.

"Did I say white knight?" she asked, as if she hadn't heard herself call Everett that. "I meant

Don Quixote, not white knight. I always manage to get those two mixed up," she said.

"I've been called worse," he said with a tolerant laugh.

Their server returned with their glasses of water and a basket of garlic breadsticks. "I'll be back with your dinners soon," she told them, placing the items on the table and withdrawing.

Everett noticed that Lila immediately picked up her glass of water. Drinking, she practically drained the entire contents in one long swallow.

Seeing that Everett was watching her, Lila shrugged self-consciously. "I guess I was thirstier than I thought."

"I guess you were," he agreed good-naturedly. Something was up, but he wasn't about to press. He didn't want to ruin their dinner. Spending time with Lila like this was far too precious to him. Having taken a breadstick, he pushed the basket toward her. "Have one. They're still warm."

He watched her take a breadstick, but instead of taking a bite, she just put it on her plate and left it there, untouched.

"What's wrong?" he asked. "You always loved breadsticks, especially garlic breadsticks."

"I still do," she answered defensively. And then she relented. "I guess I'm just not hungry."

Something was definitely off. "I've been with you all day. You haven't eaten since you came in—that's assuming that you *did* eat before you came in this morning."

Lila shrugged, then grew annoyed with herself for doing it. She wished that he'd stop asking questions. Most of all, she wished that she was home in bed.

"I'm not hungry," she snapped. "What do you want me to say?"

This was *not* like her. His eyes met hers. "The truth," Everett told her simply.

"I don't know what you're talking about," Lila retorted, irritated. "I'm just not hungry. That's not a crime," she protested.

It felt as if her emotions were going every which way at the same time.

"Look, maybe we should—"

Without thinking, Lila started to get up— which was when the world decided to launch itself into a tailspin all around her. She grabbed the edge of the table, afraid that she would suddenly go down and find herself unceremoniously sitting on the floor. The table wobbled as she grabbed it and she stifled a cry, sitting down again.

Everett reached across the table and put the back of his hand against her forehead. Lila pulled her head away. She regretted the movement immediately because the spinning in her head just intensified.

Her forehead was hot, Everett thought. That and the sharp intake of breath he'd just heard her make gave him all the input he needed.

"Dinner is canceled," he told her. "I'm taking you home and putting you to bed."

"If that's your idea of a seductive proposition, you just washed out," she informed him, struggling very hard to keep the world in focus.

"No, that's my idea of putting a sick woman to bed where she belongs." He looked around and signaled to the server. The latter was just approaching them with their orders. "Change of plans," he told her. "We have to leave."

Without missing a beat, the young woman told him, "I can have these wrapped to go in a few minutes."

Everett was about to tell the woman that they

wouldn't be taking the meals home with them, but then he had a change of heart. Lila was going to need something to eat once she was feeling better. As for him, he *was* hungry and he could always take the food to eat later once he had Lila situated.

"There's an extra tip in it for you if you can get it back here in two minutes," Everett told her.

Taking his words to heart, the server was gone before he finished his sentence.

"You're making a scene," Lila protested weakly.

"No," he retorted. "I'm trying to prevent making a scene. You're sick, Lila. I should have seen the signs. But I was so eager just to have dinner with you, I missed the fact that you were steadily growing paler all day."

Just then, the server returned. She had their dinners and breadsticks packed in two rather large paper sacks.

"Your salad is packed on top," she told him.

"Great." Taking out his wallet, Everett handed the young woman a twenty, then put a hundred-dollar bill on the table. "This should cover it," he told the server. When he turned to look at Lila, his concern grew. She was almost pasty. "Can you walk?"

"Of course I can," Lila retorted just before she stood up—and pitched forward.

Thanks to his quick reflexes, Everett managed to catch her just in time. Had he hesitated even for just half a second, Lila's head would have had an unfortunate meeting with the floor.

The server stared at them, wide-eyed. "Is she all right?" she asked, clearly concerned.

"She will be," Everett told her. He had perfected sounding confident, even when he wasn't. "I think she just has the flu," he added. In one clean, swift movement, he picked Lila up in his arms as if she was weightless. Turning toward the server, he requested, "If you could hand me her purse."

The woman had already gathered Lila's purse. "Don't worry, I'll take it and your dinners and follow you to your car," she volunteered. Looking at Lila, who was unconscious, she asked again, "You're sure she'll be all right?"

Reading between the lines, Everett told her,

"Don't worry, it wasn't anything she had here." Then he made his way to the front entrance.

Seeing them, the hostess at the reservation desk hurried to open the front door for them, holding it open with her back. "Is everything all right?" she asked Everett.

"She has the flu. She'll be fine," he answered crisply. "You do know how to make an exit," he whispered to Lila in a hushed voice. Speaking up, he said, "The car's right in front," directing the server who was hurrying alongside of him.

Still holding Lila in his arms, Everett managed to reach into his pocket and press the key fob to open the car doors.

The server moved quickly to open the passenger door for him, and Everett flashed a grateful smile at her. "Thank you."

The server waited until he buckled Lila into her seat, then handed the purse and the dinners she was holding to him.

"Are you sure you don't want me to call the paramedics for you?" she asked one last time, eyeing Lila.

"Very sure," Everett answered. "I'm a doctor. She's been out in the field, visiting sick people for the last two days and it looks like she came down with the flu for her trouble." Closing the door, he looked at the young woman and tried to set her mind at ease one last time. "Thanks for all your trouble—" he paused to read her name tag "—Ruth."

The young woman grinned broadly when he addressed her by her name. "My pleasure, Doctor." With that, she quickly hurried back into the restaurant.

Everett's attention was already focused on Lila. She was still unconscious. How the hell could he have missed all those signs? he thought, upbraiding himself again.

"I'm sorry, Lila. I should have realized what was wrong this morning in the parking lot."

And then it suddenly occurred to him that he had no idea where Lila lived. Getting her purse, he went through it until he found her wallet with her driver's license in it. Looking at it, he repeated her address out loud in order to memorize it.

"Let's get you home, Cinderella."

CHAPTER TEN

EVERETT WAS ABLE to locate the development where Lila lived with only a minimum of difficulty.

Finding her house was a little trickier. Driving slowly and trying to make out the addresses painted on the curb, he finally drove up toward her house.

Pulling up into her driveway, he turned off his engine and then sat in the car, looking at Lila. She hadn't come to once during the entire trip from the restaurant to her house.

"Okay, I got you here. Now what?" he wondered out loud. "The logical step would be to get you *into* the house, wouldn't it?" Everett said as if he was carrying on a conversation with the unconscious woman sitting next to him. "But for that to happen, I'm going to need either a roommate who's living in your house or a key to the front door."

He looked back toward the house. There weren't any lights on, which meant that either Lila lived alone, or if she did have a roommate—which she hadn't mentioned—the roommate was out.

He opened her purse again. This time he was rummaging through the purse looking for her keys. He found a set of keys at the very bottom of her purse. There were five keys on the ring.

"You sure don't make things easy, do you, Lila?" he asked.

He decided he needed to find the right key and open the front door before carrying her out of his car. If he was lucky, she might even wake up by the time he discovered which of the keys fit the front door lock. And awake, she might be able to walk—with some help—to the house. That would eliminate some complications, like nosy neighbors, he thought.

Everett went up the front walk to her door and patiently started trying out keys.

The very last key turned out to be the one to open her front door.

"It figures," he murmured.

Everett went inside the house and flipped on

the first light switch he found. The darkness receded.

At least he could find his way around, he thought.

Leaving the front door standing open, he pocketed the key ring and went back to the car.

Lila was still unconscious.

Unbuckling her seat belt, Everett found that the clothes she was wearing were all practically soaked.

"You're sweating this flu out," he told her. "As a doctor, I know that's a good thing. But I'd still feel a lot better if you opened your eyes." He looked at her, half hoping that the sound of his voice would somehow make her come around. But it didn't. "Nothing, huh?" He sighed.

The next moment, Everett took her purse and slung the straps onto his shoulder. Then he lifted her up carefully and carried her to her front door.

"If any of your neighbors are watching this, Lila, we should be hearing the sound of police sirens approaching very shortly. For both our sakes, I hope you have the kind of neighbors who keep their curtains drawn and mind their own business, at least this one time."

The wind had caused the door to close a little but he managed to shoulder it open.

Like a groom carrying his bride over the threshold, he carried Lila into the house. Once inside, he closed the door with his back, making a mental note to lock it as soon as he found some place to put Lila down.

Looking around, Everett found himself standing in a small, sparsely decorated living room.

"You never were one for a lot of possessions," he commented, scanning the room.

He saw a tan sectional sofa facing a medium-size flat-screen TV mounted on the opposite wall. Crossing over to it, Everett gently placed Lila on the sofa, leaving her there for the moment. Going back, he locked the front door and then walked around the single-story house, orienting himself. Like the living room, everything was in place and neatly arranged.

"Anyone here?" Everett called out, although he took the darkened state of the house to indicate that it was empty.

He continued to make his way through the

house, looking into each room. There were two bedrooms located in the back across from one another. One was larger than the other. He took the smaller one to be a guest bedroom. Looking into it, he found that it was empty. There were no clothes in the closet.

Apparently, Lila did live alone.

His smile vanished after a moment. This wasn't good, he thought. She was sick and she needed someone here to take care of her.

With a sigh, he went back to the living room. She was right where he'd left her—and still unconscious. He thought of his medical bag in his trunk.

"First things first," he told himself. Picking Lila up again, he said to her, "I need to get you out of these wet clothes and into bed." He caught himself smiling as he carried her to what he had determined to be her bedroom. "There was a time that would have meant something entirely different. But don't worry, I've got my 'doctor hat' on and you have nothing to worry about."

As attracted as he still was to her, his first

thought was about her health. He wanted to get Lila well again.

Bringing Lila into the larger bedroom, he managed to move aside the comforter and put her down on the queen-size bed. He took off her shoes and then began going through the drawers of her bureau, looking for a nightgown or something that looked as if she wore it to bed.

Moving a few things aside, he froze when he came across an old college jersey.

His old college jersey.

He remembered when he'd given it to her. He'd told her that when she wore it, she'd be close to him. Taking it out now, he looked at the jersey for a long moment, then at her.

"You actually kept it," he said in disbelief. "And judging by how faded it is, you've been wearing it. Maybe this isn't as hopeless as I thought," he murmured under his breath, referring to his plan to get back together with her.

Moving quickly, Everett removed the rest of her clothes and slipped the college jersey on her. Done, he tucked Lila into bed as if he was tucking in a child. He refused to allow himself to become distracted. Right now, Lila was his patient, not the only woman he had ever loved.

"I'll be right back," he told her even though she was still unconscious and couldn't hear him. "I'm going to bring in the food and get my medical bag out of the trunk."

He was back in a few minutes, leaving the to-go bags on the kitchen table for the time being. He had something far more important on his mind than food, despite the fact that his stomach kept rumbling in protest over being neglected.

Opening up his medical bag, Everett took out his stethoscope and several other basic instruments he never went anywhere without. Then he gave Lila a quick but thorough exam to confirm what he pretty much already suspected.

Her pulse was rapid, her temperature was high and, at one point, as he conducted his examination, she began to shiver.

"Chills," he noted. "And you were already displaying signs of fatigue this morning. You, Lila Clark, are a regular poster child for the flu," he concluded. Setting aside his stethoscope, he frowned. "I bet with all that running around you were doing, you forgot to get yourself immunized for the flu, didn't you?"

Mentally crossing his fingers, he looked through his bag and found that he had thought to pack some extra acetaminophen. Taking out a fresh syringe, he removed the plastic casing and gave her an injection.

"That should help lower your fever," he told Lila. He frowned thoughtfully. "But you still can't be left alone, not like this."

There was a chair over in the corner by the window and he dragged it over to her bed. Sitting down, Everett studied her for a few minutes, reviewing his options. He was due back in Houston tomorrow, but there was no way he was about to leave her in this condition.

The injection he gave her should lower her fever, but things didn't always go the way they were supposed to. If Lila took a turn for the worse, there was no one here to take her to the hospital. Or do anything else for her, for that matter.

Even if he didn't feel the way he did about her, he couldn't just abandon her.

Everett made up his mind. He might not have

been there for Lila thirteen years ago, but he could be here for her now.

Stepping out into the hallway, he took out his cell phone and placed a call to one of the doctors he worked with. He found himself listening to an answering machine telling him to leave a message. He'd hoped to talk to the other man directly, but that wasn't an option right now.

"Ryan, it's Everett. I'm in the middle of some sort of flu epidemic here in Austin and I'm going to be staying here a few more days. I'm going to need you and Blake to cover for me at the office. I appreciate it and I owe you—big time. Any questions, you have my cell."

With that, he terminated the call.

Coming back into the room to check on Lila, Everett called Schuyler next. His sister answered on the second ring.

"Schuy, it's Everett. I'm going to be staying in Austin a few more days."

"Oh?" Schuyler really didn't sound all that surprised, he thought. "Did you and Lila manage to patch things up?" she asked.

He wasn't about to get into that right now.

That was a personal matter and it was officially on the back burner until Lila got well.

"It's not what you think," Everett was quick to tell his sister.

"Okay, if you're not trying to romance Lila into taking you back, then why are you going to be staying in Austin a few more days?" Schuyler wanted to know.

"You know that flu epidemic I came here to help treat?"

"Yes, I got my vaccination, Ev," she told him, thinking that was what her brother was going to ask her.

"Good, but that wasn't what I was about to tell you," Everett said.

"Okay, then what were you going to tell me?" Schuyler asked gamely.

"Lila came down with the flu," he told his sister simply. "She lives by herself and there's no one to take care of her."

"My Lord," Schuyler cried. "If I saw this story on one of those movie-of-the-week channels I'd shut off the TV."

"I didn't ask for your evaluation," Everett told

her impatiently. "I just wanted you to know that I was still in town—and why."

After a moment, Schuyler said, "You're serious. Then she's really sick?"

Did Schuyler think that Lila would pretend to be ill—and that he'd just blindly fall for it?

"Schuy, I'm a doctor. I know what 'sick' looks like. Right now, Lila's not only displaying all the signs of the flu, she's unconscious."

Schuyler's tone of voice changed immediately. "Anything I can do?"

He thought of Lila's car. It was still at the Foundation's parking lot where Lila had left it. He knew that Lila would undoubtedly prefer to have the car close by when she regained consciousness—if for no other reason than there might be something in it that she needed.

"As a matter of fact, there is," Everett told her. "If you and one of your friends could swing by here tomorrow morning to get the keys, could you pick up Lila's car from the Foundation's parking lot and drive it over to her house?"

"I think I liked you better when you didn't feel it was seemly to ask for favors," Schuyler told him.

He knew she was kidding. He also knew he could count on his sister.

"I'm growing as a person," Everett quipped.

"That's not how I see it," she told him. "All right, where's 'here'?" his sister asked.

He thought he heard her shuffling papers on the other end and then he heard Schuler say, "Okay, give me Lila's address."

He did, and then he said, "I assume you know where the Fortune Foundation is located."

"You know, you can be very insulting, big brother," Schuyler told him.

"Not intentionally," he told her, then added, "Thanks for this, Schuy."

"Yeah. I just hope you're not going to wind up regretting this, that's all," she told him, sounding concerned.

She was worried and he appreciated that. But there was no need for his sister to feel that way. "Schuy, Lila's sick. I'm a doctor. I'm supposed to take care of sick people."

Schuyler barely stifled a laugh. "You don't think this a little above and beyond?" she questioned.

"I'm an 'above and beyond' kind of doctor,"

Everett answered, doing his best to make light of the concerns his sister was displaying.

"Not funny, Ev," Schuyler informed him. "I worry about you," she stressed.

"And I said I appreciate that. I also appreciate you picking up that car and bringing it back to Lila's house for me," he said, bringing the conversation back to what he was asking her to do.

Schuyler sighed. "What time do you want me to come by?"

There was no reason to push. "Whenever it's convenient." He glanced toward Lila's room. "It doesn't look as if I'm going to be going anywhere for at least a while."

"I'll still call you first," she told Everett. It was obvious that she wasn't going to take a chance on walking in on something.

Everett was just about to end the call when he heard his sister say his name. Bringing the cell phone closer again so he could hear her, he asked, "Did you just say something?"

"I just had a last-minute thought," she told him.

"And that is?"

His sister hesitated for a moment. "I don't

suppose I can talk you into hiring someone to look after Lila, can I?"

He knew she was just thinking of him, but he wished she would stop. He wanted to do this and his mind was made up.

"I'll see you in the morning, Schuyler," he said just before he terminated the call.

Putting the phone back into his pocket, he returned to Lila's bedside.

When he touched her forehead, it seemed a little cooler to him. Taking out the thermometer he'd used earlier, he laid the strip across her forehead and watched the numbers registering.

He removed the strip and put it back into his medical bag.

"You still have a fever," he told her. "But at least it's a little lower. Although not low enough," he stressed with a frown. "You can't go out and do your angel-of-mercy bit until that fever is gone and you're back to your old self again."

Lila moaned.

He knew it wasn't in response to what he'd just said, but he pretended that there was a semblance of an exchange going on between the two of them.

Lila had a small TV in her bedroom. Nothing like the one in the living room, but at least it would be something to fill the silence and distract him, he thought.

Turning on the TV, he put the volume on low, sat down in the chair next to Lila's bed and made himself as comfortable as possible.

He knew he could make use of the guest room and lie down on the bed there, but he preferred proximity over comfort. He wanted to be there for her if Lila woke up in the middle of the night and needed him. One night in a chair wouldn't kill him.

Besides, how many nights had he gone without sleep when he was an intern at the hospital? That certainly hadn't done him any harm, Everett reminded himself—and neither would spending a night sitting up and keeping vigil in a chair.

Everett doubted that he would get any sleep in the guest room anyway. He knew himself. He'd be too busy straining his ears, listening for any strange noises that would indicate that Lila was awake.

No, he decided, trying to make himself as comfortable as possible in the chair. Staying in Lila's room this way was better. He'd be right here, able to hear her make the slightest sound when she woke up. And he figured she *had* to wake up soon.

"I know you need your rest so I'm not going to worry about this yet. But I'd take it as a personal favor if you opened those big blue eyes of yours soon, Lila. *Very* soon."

The only response he heard was the sound of Lila breathing.

CHAPTER ELEVEN

"WHAT ARE YOU doing in my house?"

The raspy voice was hardly louder than a hoarse whisper, but it was definitely unnerving and accusatory in nature. Catching Everett off guard, it made him jump in his chair and almost caused him to knock it over.

Coming to, Everett realized that he must have finally dozed off for a few minutes.

It took him a moment longer before it hit him that it was Lila who'd asked the question.

Fully awake now, he got up and stood over Lila's bed. Her eyes were open and she looked bewildered. Relief washed over him as he took her hand in his. "You're awake!"

"And you didn't answer my question," Lila responded, annoyed with herself because she couldn't seem to speak any louder. "What are you doing in my house?" she asked again.

Bits and pieces were slowly beginning to

dawn on her. She looked down at herself. "And where are my clothes?" Her eyes narrowed as she looked up at Everett angrily. "You undressed me," Lila choked out. It was not a question.

Everett wasn't about to deny the obvious, but she needed to understand why he'd removed her clothes. "You had a high fever and you were sweating. Your clothes were soaked straight through."

Frustration robbed her of the little voice she had so she couldn't immediately respond. She struggled to sit up.

All Everett had to do was put his hand gently on her shoulder to keep her down, which he did. "Don't exert yourself," he told her.

Who the hell did he think he was? He couldn't tell her what to do, Lila thought angrily. Her head was throbbing and she couldn't remember anything. But one thing was obvious.

"You took off my clothes," she accused again.

"I already explained why," Everett told her patiently.

She couldn't make any sense out of what he'd told her. "But we were in the restaurant," she protested, desperately trying to piece things together. It felt as if there was a huge gaping hole in her brain and facts were just falling through it, disappearing without a trace.

Maybe if he gave her a summary of the events, Everett thought, it might calm her down.

"You passed out in the restaurant," he told her. "I brought you to your house and carried you to your room. Your clothes were all wet, so I got you out of them and into that jersey."

She looked down again, doing her best to focus on what she was looking at. The jersey seemed to swim in front of her eyes. "You went through my things," she accused.

"Just in order to find something to put on you," he answered simply. Maybe he should have let it go at that, but he couldn't help saying, "You kept my jersey."

She wasn't about to get into that—and she wouldn't have had to if he hadn't gone rummaging through her drawers, she thought angrily.

"You had no right to go through my things," she said defensively.

This was going nowhere. He wasn't about to get sucked into a circular debate about what he'd done and why he'd done it.

"Lila, you have the flu. The best thing for you right now is to rest and drink plenty of fluids. Arguing is not part of that formula. Now I'll get you some water—or tea if you'd prefer. Your job in this is to take care of the 'rest' part."

Lila made a disgruntled face. "I don't like tea," she told him.

"Water it is," he responded, heading out to the kitchen.

A couple of minutes later Everett came back with a large glass of water. He propped her up with one hand beneath her pillows while he held out the glass to her with the other.

Lila took the glass with both hands and began to drink with gusto.

"Sip, don't gulp," he cautioned.

"I know how to drink water," she informed him, her voice still raspy. However, she grudgingly complied with his instructions. Getting her fill, she surrendered the glass.

Taking it from her, Everett slowly lowered her back down on the bed.

Lila's head felt as if it was floating and there were half thoughts darting in and out of her brain. Her eyes shifted in his direction.

"Did you enjoy it?" she asked.

His back was to her as he put the glass down on the bureau. Turning around, Everett looked at her quizzically. He had no idea what she was referring to. "Did I enjoy what?"

"Undressing me."

Her voice was even lower than it had been before and he could hardly make out what she was saying. He filled in the blanks.

"I did it in my capacity as a doctor," Everett answered.

Confusion furrowed her brow. Nothing was making sense. "Meaning you didn't look?"

Everett had deliberately divorced himself from his feelings while he'd gotten her out of the wet clothes and into the jersey. But not enough to be completely unaffected by what he was doing. However, he wasn't about to tell her that. That would have been deliberately buying trouble in his opinion.

Instead, he said, "Only to make sure I didn't rip anything."

Her eyes narrowed further as she tried to look into his. "I don't think I believe you," she whispered.

The next moment, her eyes had closed and within a few seconds, she was asleep again.

"That's okay," he whispered back, gently pushing her hair away from her face and tucking her back under the covers. "I wouldn't believe me either if I were you."

He'd gotten her out of her clothes and into the jersey as quickly as he could, but that didn't mean that doing so hadn't stirred something within him even though he had tried his damnedest to block out those thoughts and feelings.

He *had* been functioning as a doctor, but he was remembering as her lover and that image was really difficult to shake.

The next time Lila opened her eyes and looked around, she saw that she was alone.

It had all been a dream, she thought with a twinge of disappointment.

She struggled into an upright position, her body aching and protesting every movement she made.

She stifled a groan. She felt as if she'd been run over by a truck. A truck that had deliberately backed up over her then taken off after running her over again.

She struggled to focus, her head throbbing, impeding her thoughts.

How did she get here? The last thing she actually remembered was being in the restaurant—sitting opposite Everett.

Everett had been part of her dream, she realized.

All these years and she was still having dreams about Everett. Strange dreams.

She needed to get up, she thought.

Just as she was about to throw back her covers, Everett walked into the room carrying a tray.

He smiled, pleased to see her up. "You're awake."

Lila's mouth dropped open as she stared at him. "I didn't dream you."

He set the tray down on the bureau for the moment.

"You dreamt about me?" he asked. He was practically beaming.

She became instantly defensive. "What are you doing here?"

"We went through this last night," he reminded her patiently. "Don't you remember?"

"I thought that was a dream." She was repeating herself, Lila thought. She held her head. It was really throbbing. "I feel awful."

"Well, if it makes you feel any better, you don't look awful," he told her. "But you are sick."

"No, I'm not," she protested. She tried to throw the covers off again and found that the single movement was exceedingly taxing to her strength. What the hell had happened to her? "I have to get ready for work," she told Everett defiantly, wanting him to leave.

Everett carefully drew her covers back up. "No work for you until you get well," he told her, leaving no room for argument.

Didn't he understand? "I've got people counting on me," she told him.

"And if you turn up, you'll be *infecting* those people." She tried to get up again and this time, he held down her hands just enough to keep her where she was. "Are you familiar with the story of Typhoid Mary?"

Was that what Everett thought she was? A

woman who wantonly infected people? "That's not funny."

"I'm not trying to be funny, Lila," he told her. "But I am trying to get through to you. You're sick." Everett told her, enunciating every word slowly. "You have the flu."

She felt like hell warmed over, but she still protested, "No, I don't."

His eyes met hers. "Which one of us went to medical school?" he asked her in a quiet, tolerant voice that only served to infuriate her.

She blew out an angry breath. "You did," she said grudgingly.

Everett smiled. She had made his point for him. "You have the flu," he repeated.

"I can't have the flu," she insisted. She looked up at Everett, her eyes pleading with him.

This had to be good, he thought. "Why?"

Exasperation throbbed in every syllable. "Because I just can't."

Everett decided to play along as if she had a valid argument that needed exploration. "Did you get vaccinated?"

"No," Lila admitted, mumbling the word under her breath.

A triumphant look slipped over his face. "Okay, all together now: You have the flu."

Defeated, Lila sank back onto her pillow as if all the air had been suddenly pumped out of her.

"I really have the flu?" Lila asked him, silently begging him to come up with another explanation.

Rather than answer her immediately, Everett decided to back himself up with evidence. "What's your throat feel like?"

She didn't have to think before answering. "Sandpaper."

"And your head?" he asked, giving her a chance to contradict his diagnosis.

It was getting harder and harder for her to focus because of the pain. "Like there're twelve angry elves with steel hammers in it trying to beat their way out."

"Add that to the chills I observed last night and the high fever—which by the way is going down—and you have more than your fair share of flu symptoms."

"The flu," Lila repeated in despair, saying it as if it was the mark of Cain on her forehead.

"Isn't there anything you can do for me?" she asked, almost pleading with him.

"I'm doing it," he told her. "I'm nursing you back to health with bed rest, liquids and I have here a bowl of chicken soup that's guaranteed to cure what ails you," he quipped.

He'd found a folding TV tray tucked away in one of the closets and he set it up now next to her bed. When he was satisfied that it was stable, he put the bowl of soup on it along with a large soupspoon.

"See if you can hold that down," he told her.

Lila looked down into the bowl of soup as if she was trying to make up her mind about it. "Chicken soup?" she repeated.

"Highly underrated, by the way," he told her. "Apparently, our grandmothers knew something about its healing powers that we didn't. Seriously," he told Lila. "Try taking a few spoonfuls," he urged, helping her sit up and placing two pillows at her back to keep her upright.

The spoon was in her hand, but it remained motionless for now. "Where did you get the soup?" she asked. She knew she didn't have any canned soups in her kitchen cabinets.

"I had Schuyler bring it," he answered. He'd called his sister this morning and added that to his first request. "Along with your car," Everett said.

"My car?" Lila repeated. And then it suddenly came back to her. "My car's at the Foundation." Panic had entered her voice.

"Not anymore. Schuyler and her fiancé swung by this morning to pick up the keys to your car. They already drove it over. It's right outside in your driveway," he told her.

Lila looked at him in wonder. "You took care of everything," she marveled.

Everett grinned. "What can I say? I'm an overachiever."

Lila smiled at his choice of words. "I remember that about you," she said with almost a fond note in her voice.

When she sounded like that, he could feel himself melting. Now wasn't the time. "Eat your soup before it gets cold," he urged.

"And loses its magic healing powers?" she asked in an amused voice that was finally beginning to sound more like her.

"Something like that."

Lila nodded. "All right, I'll eat—if you tell me exactly what happened last night," she bargained.

"I already told you," he said. Seeing that she wasn't about to budge until he'd told her the whole story without skipping anything, Everett sighed. "But I'll tell you again," he said, resigned. "We were at the restaurant and you suddenly passed out."

She visualized that now and became horrified. "In front of everybody?"

"Just the people looking our way," he quipped. "I didn't take a head count," he said, doing his best not to get her agitated.

"Nobody called the paramedics, did they?" Lila asked. The last thing she wanted was for this to get around. She wanted to be able to do her job when she got back, not have to constantly be answering a lot of questions because there were rumors circulating about her. Rumors always had a way of escalating and becoming exaggerated.

The thought of having to deal with that made her feel more ill.

"Well, you frightened the server, but I told her I was a doctor and that seemed to satisfy her. So I picked you up and carried you to my car. Our waitress followed us with your purse and the dinners she packed up to go—which, by the way, are in the refrigerator waiting for you once you get your appetite back."

"How did you know where I lived?" Lila asked suddenly. She hadn't told him her address.

"I got it from your driver's license in your purse," he told her. "Which, before you ask, is where I found the keys to your house. And the car," he added, "so that Schuyler could drive it here. Okay," he informed her, "that about catches us up."

Turning, he was about to return to the kitchen when she cried, "Wait."

Now what? He did his best not to sound impatient. "I told you everything," he stressed.

"Weren't you supposed to go back to your practice in Houston today?" she asked, remembering he'd said something to that effect.

He looked at her pointedly. Was she trying to get him to make some sort of a declaration about the way he felt about her, or was this just an innocent question? "My plans changed."

"You don't have to stay here on my account," she protested.

"Lila, right now a pregnant cat could beat you at arm wrestling with one paw tied behind her back. You have the strength of an overcooked noodle. You need to rest and you need someone to take care of you while you're resting. I'm volunteering."

She shook her head and almost instantly regretted it. Her head started swimming and she waited for it to steady itself again. "I can't let you do that."

"I don't recall asking for permission," he told her. "I've got more vacation time coming to me than any two people in my office combined and I'm electing to take some of it now. Now don't argue with me. Eat your soup and lie back, watch some mindless TV and rest. Doctor's orders," he added when she opened her mouth to protest. "Understood?"

Looking somewhat subdued, which both surprised and worried him, Lila repeated, "Understood."

CHAPTER TWELVE

SHE REMEMBERED.

Although Lila tried very hard not to, over the course of the next few days she began to remember why she had fallen in love with Everett to begin with. Not because he was so devastatingly handsome—which he still was, perhaps even more so—but because he was so kind.

Kind and thoughtful and caring.

She'd witnessed those traits in action while accompanying Everett on the house calls they'd paid together before she'd gotten ill, and now she was witnessing it up close and personal while he was taking care of her and nursing her back to health.

In essence, Everett was very quietly waiting on her hand and foot. He made sure she drank plenty of fluids. He prepared a soft, bland diet for her, then slowly substituted food with more substance when he felt she could handle it. The progression took close to a week because he told her he didn't want to rush things and risk her having a setback.

By the end of the fourth day of her convalescence, Lila had gotten comfortable enough with him to allow herself to share a few old stories about people they had known back in high school.

Since she had left Houston thirteen years ago, he was in a far better position to tell her what some of the people they had grown up with were doing these days.

"Remember Jack Logan?" Everett asked, bringing up another name as they were sharing a lunch of soup and sandwiches in her room.

It took Lila a moment to put a face to the name. "Oh, you mean the guy who expected every woman to faint at his feet just because he looked their way?" She remembered that Jack was always telling everyone he had big plans for himself. "Whatever happened to him?"

Everett smiled, remembering how brash and abrasive Logan had been. "He still lives in Houston and works at the airport as a baggage checker."

As she recalled, that didn't exactly match up to Logan's lofty goals. "Is he still a lady-killer?"

He looked at Lila and answered her with a straight face. "Only if he fell on top of one. I saw him recently. He must have gained over a hundred pounds since graduation."

Lila tried to stifle a laugh, but she couldn't help herself. Somehow, that seemed like poetic justice. Logan had always been cruelly critical of anyone he felt wasn't as good-looking as he was. His remarks were always particularly hurtful about women he viewed to be over-weight, even if they were carrying only a few extra pounds.

"He was always such an egotist," she said when she stopped laughing.

"That part hasn't changed," Everett told her. Finishing his meal, he wiped his mouth and put down his napkin. "I think he just sees his ex-panding weight as there being more of him to be impressed with." He looked at Lila's plate. "Are you finished?" he asked, nodding at her tray.

"Yes." As Everett removed the tray, she told

him, "You know, you really don't have to wait on me hand and foot like this."

For the time being, Everett placed the tray aside on the bureau. He could take both trays to the kitchen the next time he left the room.

"Well, I'm here and there's not that much else to do," he reasoned. "So, to my way of thinking, I might as well make myself useful."

"That's another thing," she said, picking up on the fact that he was still in Austin. "I'm keeping you from your practice."

His eyes met hers for a long moment. And then he said, "Maybe I like being kept."

Lila felt herself growing warm and she didn't think that she was having any sort of a relapse. At least not the kind that involved the flu.

She did her best to steer the conversation in the initial direction she'd intended.

"What I'm saying is that you don't need to take care of me anymore. I'm getting better all the time."

"That's because of all the excellent care you've been getting."

Lila smiled, shaking her head. Everett had

always had a way with words. "I won't argue with that."

"Good," Everett said with finality. He had brought her that day's TV schedule earlier for her to look through. He picked it up now and thumbed through it. "Now what would you like to watch this afternoon?" he asked. Watching TV after lunch had become a ritual for them the last few days, something he felt that they both looked forward to. "There're some pretty good old movies on the Classic Channel and I found a station that's streaming a lot of those old sitcoms you used to like watching." He named a couple of specific programs.

Hearing them cited, Lila looked at him in surprise. "You remember that?" she marveled.

"I remember a lot of things," he told her. He had committed a great many things to memory about her, Everett thought.

Lila could feel her heart racing even though she fiercely ordered it not to. She'd been this route before and she knew exactly where it ended. Nowhere, leaving her with an ache in her heart. She did *not* want to go there, not again.

But somehow, she just couldn't seem to convince herself to turn away, to choose a different path. She tried to assuage her conscience by telling herself that this was only for a little while.

Lila shrugged in response to his question. "I don't know, you pick something," she told him. The next moment, she threw back her covers and swung her legs down. "I'll be right back."

"Where are you going?"

"I need to use the bathroom," she informed him with as much dignity as she could muster.

All the other times she'd felt the need to go, Everett had taken her arm and walked her to the bathroom as if they were out for an evening stroll. It was obvious to him that this time around, Lila was attempting to assert her independence. Not that he could blame her. In her place, he'd try to do the same thing.

Everett took a step back, allowing her space so she could get out of bed. However, he still kept a watchful eye on her.

On her feet now, he could see that Lila was still rather unstable. She took a single step and her right knee buckled.

Everett's arms were around her instantly, keeping her from landing on the floor. When he drew her back up, her body slid ever so slightly against his.

It was only for a second, but it was enough. Enough to send sparks flying between them and throwing old longings into high gear.

Everett caught his breath, silently ordering himself to remain steady instead of pulling her closer to him and kissing her the way he wanted to.

Instead of making love with her the way he desperately wanted to.

Only extreme self-control kept him from acting on the impulses that were urgently telegraphing themselves throughout his whole body.

"I know you wanted to do this alone, but maybe I should just walk with you to the bathroom this one more time," he suggested.

"To keep me from doing a pratfall?" she asked ruefully.

Her ego stood as much of a chance of being hurt as her body, so he tactfully rephrased what she'd just asked. "So you don't risk bruising anything if you do happen to fall," he told her. "So, is it okay?" he asked, waiting for her to give him the go-ahead on this.

She sighed and then smiled at him. She realized Everett was trying to spare her feelings. "Well, the old saying is that pride always goes before a fall and I don't want to fall, so I guess I'll have to just tuck away my pride and let you walk me to the bathroom one more time."

Everett laughed softly. "Good call," he congratulated her. "You'll be doing solo runs again before you know it," he promised.

Sitting on the edge of Lila's bed, Everett set aside his stethoscope. He'd just finished giving Lila her latest examination.

"Well, your fever's gone," he told her. "You're keeping your food down and your color's definitely back. And when you talk, you no longer sound like someone who starts their mornings with a shot of scotch and a cigarette. Although I have to say that I was getting kind of used to hearing that sexy voice. I might actually miss it," he admitted, smiling fondly at her.

"Well, I won't," Lila assured him with feeling. "I thought I sounded like some kidnapper placing a ransom call." She looked at him hopefully. "Does this mean that I'm being cleared for work?"

Everett nodded. He closed his medical bag and set it on the floor.

"Our little unofficial holiday is over," he told her, then in case there was any doubt, he added, "Yes, I'm clearing you for work."

Lila didn't take her eyes off him. "And you'll be going back to Houston?"

"I will," Everett confirmed. He knew he had to be getting back, but there was a part of him that didn't want to leave.

If he were honest with himself, he'd admit that he'd used nursing Lila back to health as an excuse to spend more time with her.

The last thirteen years had been filled with work, at times almost nonstop. He knew now that he had been trying to fill the emptiness— the gaping void that losing her had created— with work. Work and the occasional woman. None of them ever measured up to Lila simply because no one had ever even come close to making him feel the way Lila had.

The way she still did.

"But I'll still be coming back to Austin a lot," he told her, never breaking eye contact. "To see Schuyler and help her out with some things," he added, not wanting to scare Lila off. He paused for a moment, then, despite the advice Schuyler had given him, he asked, "Is it all right if I call you when I'm in town?"

After the way that he had put himself out for her, she hadn't expected Everett to ask permission to call her. She assumed he'd think he'd earned the right to call her any time he wanted to.

"How can I say no to the man who nursed me back to health?" she asked, trying to sound as if she was amused by his question.

"I'm not asking you to see me as the man who nursed you back to health," Everett pointed out. "I'm asking you to see me—" he paused for a moment, looking for the right phrasing "—as an old friend."

The silence between them grew until she finally said to him, "I couldn't say no to that, either."

"Glad to hear it," he told her.

He let out the breath he'd been holding. Honestly, he really hadn't known what Lila would say in response to his question. He wouldn't have put it past her feelings of self-preservation to tell him that seeing each other again wouldn't be a good idea.

But now that she had agreed, he saw that there was something far greater than self-preservation going on between them.

He could feel it.

And it was not just on his end. Nor was it just wishful thinking.

There was something tangible and real pulsating between them, ready to spring to life at the slightest bit of encouragement.

But even with all that, Everett knew he had to tread lightly. One wrong step and it could all crumble right beneath him, sending him plummeting head first into an abyss.

"Hi, are you free for dinner tonight?"

"Everett?" Lila was immediately alert. She'd answered her cell phone just as she'd walked in her front door, thinking it was someone at the Foundation working late, calling with a question.

But it wasn't.

"I didn't expect to hear from you this soon," she said.

It had been six days since she had gone back to work and he had returned to Houston.

"Well, I'm only in Austin for a few hours," he explained, "so I thought, if you're free, you might want to get together."

There it was, she thought. Her way out. He was handing it to her.

If you're free.

That was all she had to say to him. That she wasn't free. That her evening was already spoken for and she had somewhere else to be. And knowing Everett, he would accept that, murmur his regrets and that would be that.

The problem was, she didn't want to take this way out that he was handing her on a silver platter. She *wanted* to see him. The truth of it was, after seeing him every day for almost a week, she missed him.

She knew that she shouldn't feel this way. Knew that she needed to cut Everett out of her life before he became a habit. But then on the other hand, this *was* only going to be dinner. And dinner would last for a few hours at most, nothing more. She knew that Everett was far too conscientious to lie to her, especially for some ulterior motive. If he said he was only here for a few hours, then he *was* in Austin only for that time.

Those few hours might as well be spent with her, she thought in a moment of weakness.

"I am free," she heard herself saying, sealing her fate, at least for the next few hours. "We can do dinner if you like. And I promise not to pass out this time," she added with amusement, remembering the last time they were in a restaurant together.

"Oh." He pretended to sound as if he was sorry to hear that. "Too bad," he told her. "I was looking forward to playing the hero, sweeping you into my arms and carrying you to my car."

"I think being the hero once would be enough for any guy."

"Oh, I don't know," Everett speculated. "It's kind of addictive if the hero has the right damsel in distress to save."

That definitely conjured up an image, Lila thought. "I never envisioned myself as a damsel in distress," she told Everett.

"I wouldn't have thought of you as one, either," he admitted. "I guess the world is full of surprises." Then he changed topics. "Well, like I said, I'm only in Austin for a bit, so where would you like to go?"

"Seeing what happened the last time when we went to the Italian restaurant, how about Chinese food?" Lila suggested.

"Sounds good to me," he told her. He would have said the same thing if she had suggested strolling through the park, eating ice cream cones. He just wanted to see her. It had been six long days during which time he had forced himself not to call her just to see how she was doing. Or to hear the sound of her voice. He didn't want Lila to feel as if he was crowding her, or worse, as if he was stalking her.

But it hadn't been easy.

He had spent six days *with* her when she'd been ill with the flu and he had quickly gotten used to seeing her everyday. *Not* seeing her was hell now, but he couldn't behave like some privileged adolescent who was accustomed to having his every whim indulged—no matter how much he wished.

This was too important for him to risk messing up again. So he treaded lightly.

"If it's okay, I can be at your place in half an hour. Or is that too soon? Do you need more time?"

"Actually, I need less if you're close by. I just got home from work and I still look very businesslike, so I don't need to change."

He preferred the temptress look he'd seen on her, but to remain safe, he thought that it was best to go along with the business suit.

"You always look good no matter what you have on." *And sometimes even better the less you have on*, he added silently. "I'll be there in fifteen minutes."

CHAPTER THIRTEEN

LILA FELT AS if she had suddenly blinked and just like that, found herself going back to square one all over again. She was experiencing feelings of excitement and wariness and that in turn had created knots in her stomach.

Big ones.

But not quite big enough for her to call Everett and tell him that she'd changed her mind about having dinner with him.

Despite saying that she didn't need any extra time to get ready because she was still dressed for work, Lila impulsively flew into her bedroom for a quick change of clothes. She didn't want to look as if she was going to a business meeting. She wanted to look as good as she could possibly look.

Like a woman who was going out to dinner with a man who had once owned her heart.

Not that she planned on letting him own it

again, she maintained as she quickly pulled the pins out of her hair. Instantly, the changed hairstyle made her appear more carefree. Her auburn hair cascaded around her face instead of being neatly pulled back, out of the way.

Her practical attire gave way to an attractive, form-flattering dress. She had just slipped on a pair of high heels that could have never, by any stretch of the imagination, been called sensible, when she heard the doorbell ring.

The sound instantly had her heart accelerating.

Showtime, she thought.

Hurrying to the front of the house, she stopped just short of the front door in order to catch her breath. She pulled herself together, doing her best to look as if she was totally nonchalant about the evening that lay ahead of her.

Everett would probably see right through her, she thought. Even so, she felt that she still had to keep up the charade.

Taking in one more deep breath and then slowly releasing it, she opened the door.

"When you say fifteen minutes, you really

mean fifteen minutes," she said as she smiled up into Everett's handsome face.

"A man's only as good as his word," he responded. "You know, we don't have to leave right away if you're not ready yet."

"Do I look like I'm not ready yet?" she asked.

Despite her coy bravado, Lila couldn't help wondering what it was that Everett saw when he looked at her. Had he been hoping she'd be wearing something more appealing? Sexier?

Don't borrow trouble, she warned herself.

Everett's eyes slowly washed over the length of her. There was nothing but approval evident in his eyes. "You look, in a word, perfect," he pronounced.

Lila smiled at the compliment, secretly pleased although she tried her best to appear indifferent. "Then I guess I'm ready." Taking her purse, she walked out of the house, then paused to lock up.

Everett's Mercedes was waiting in her driveway.

"By the way," Everett said as he held the passenger door open for her, "I know you said we were going to a Chinese restaurant, but if I'm driving, you need to tell me the address."

She waited for Everett to get in on his side. Once he buckled up, she gave him the address, adding, "It's about half a mile past the Foundation. A lot of people from work like grabbing lunch at Gin Ling's."

Everett thought for a second. "I think I know which restaurant you mean," he told her. He remembered seeing it when he'd driven to the Foundation. "That's the one that's built to look like a pagoda, right?"

"Right."

Gin Ling's was doing brisk business when they arrived. They had to wait a few minutes to be seated.

Thinking that Everett might grow impatient, Lila told him, "We can go somewhere else if you don't want to wait."

Everett made no move to take her up on the suggestion. "Do you like eating here?" he asked her.

She wouldn't have suggested coming here if she hadn't. That wasn't the point. "Yes, but—"

"Then we'll wait," he told her, adding, "I'm

not in any hurry. I like making the most of the little downtime I get."

There was a reason why she had mentioned the idea of going to another restaurant. "I just don't want to make you late."

Everett looked at her as if he wasn't quite following her. "For what? I don't have a plane to catch," he reminded Lila. "I'm driving back to Houston."

"Doesn't all that driving make you tired?" In his place, she'd find driving back and forth between Austin and Houston exhausting after a while.

However, Everett shook his head. "On the contrary. Driving relaxes me."

Relaxing made her think about falling asleep at the wheel—not that Everett would ever admit that he was in danger of doing that. But she didn't want to think that he ran the risk of having something happen to him because of her.

"Still," she told him, "I don't want you so relaxed that you just slide right out of your seat."

"Never happen," Everett assured her. Still, her comment made his heart lighter.

She was clearly worried about him, he

thought, and that felt particularly encouraging. Because that meant that there were still feelings there. Feelings he intended to stoke and encourage.

"Don't worry," he said. "I like staying in one piece as much as the next man. If I ever feel too tired to drive back, I'll rent a motel room and sleep until I feel up to driving. And, don't forget, there's always Schuyler," he reminded her.

A hostess came to show them to their table. Lila fell into place behind the woman with Everett following right behind her.

"Sorry, I was just remembering how stubborn you could be," Lila told him as they were being shown to a cozy booth.

"Not stubborn," Everett corrected, waiting for her to slide in before taking his own seat opposite her. "Determined."

Lila smiled. "Right. Determined," she repeated, humoring him.

"So how was going back to work?" Everett asked her after their server had brought them a pot of tea and then departed after taking each of their orders.

"Wonderfully hectic as always," she told him.

But Everett was more interested in the state of her health. "You didn't have any relapses or feel any ill effects from the flu?"

"No. I didn't expect that there would be," she told him honestly, smiling at Everett. "I always knew that you would be a fantastic doctor."

Everett maintained a straight face as he nodded. "I haven't mastered walking on water yet," he deadpanned, "but I'm working on it."

About to bring the small cup of tea to her lips, Lila stopped just short of completing the action, staring at him.

Everett laughed. "Well, you were making it sound as if I'd done something extraordinary," he told her. "I just took it a step further."

"You went out of your way for a patient—which was what I was," she reminded him. "Not every doctor would have stayed with a patient for almost a week because there was no one to take care of her."

"Not just any patient," Everett pointed out, "but a patient I was once nearly engaged to."

"And that near-engagement ended badly," she reminded him. Before he could say anything in response, she went on to tell him, "You had every right in the world to call the paramedics, then have them take me to the hospital while you walked away."

He inclined his head like a man conceding a point. "Okay. You got me. I'm a magnificent doctor—who was hoping for a second chance at dinner," he added as if that had been his sole motive behind seeing to it that she got well. "In order to do that, I had to make sure that you stayed alive. The best way to do that was to see to it myself." He shrugged. "I don't delegate very well."

She paused to sample the egg roll appetizer that had been brought to the table and then laughed.

"When did you get so good at twisting around words to make them back you up?" she wanted to know.

"It comes with the medical degree," Everett responded.

"No, it doesn't," Lila countered. She felt herself verging on impatience at the way he was so dismissive of his own abilities.

"Okay, then let's just say it's an inherent talent. A gift," he emphasized. "Born out of necessity," he added. "Satisfied?" He studied her across the table.

"No," Lila answered honestly. "But I guess that it'll have to do for now."

She was rewarded with a smile that seemed to come from deep inside of Everett. She could feel her heart flutter in response.

They talked for another hour, long after the main course and the fortune cookies had come and gone and the pot of tea had been refilled.

"I think we'd better get going. It looks like our server wants the table." She looked toward the reception area and saw why. "There's a line going all out the door now."

Everett found himself reluctant to leave. "I'm sure I can find a way to make it up to him if you want to stay a little longer. Would you like a few more appetizers?" he asked.

Lila laughed. "If I so much as look at another one, I'll explode."

"Okay, that's a no," he acknowledged. "So I guess you're ready to go?"

Lila nodded. "I've got another day at work tomorrow and you, you've got a long drive ahead of you," she reminded him. "I can call a cab for myself if you'd like to get started on that drive home," Lila offered, watching Everett's expression for any indication that he did want to leave.

Everett regarded her thoughtfully. "If I didn't know any better, I would venture to say that you were trying to get rid of me."

"No," Lila denied, saying the word with feeling. "I'm not."

He grinned at her. "Good, because it's not working. I'm going to be taking you home. The few extra minutes that it'll take me isn't going to make a difference as far as my trip is concerned," he assured her. Raising his hand, he signaled to the server.

True to his word, Everett left an extra large tip on the table for the man. Large enough to prompt their server to call after them as they left, saying, "Please come again!"

Lila and Everett exchanged looks and grinned at one another just before they walked out of the increasingly crowded restaurant.

"I had a really nice time tonight," she told Everett once she was at her door.

Everett nodded, doing his best to look solemn as he reviewed their evening.

"Well, you made it all the way back home without passing out, so the way I see it, it was a successful evening," he said dryly.

Lila shook her head. "You're not going to let me live that down, are you?" she asked.

"In time, maybe," he conceded.

Key in hand, Lila stopped just short of putting it into the lock. She knew she was stalling, but she couldn't help herself.

"Does that mean you want to do this again?" she asked Everett.

"Absolutely," Everett answered with certainly. He paused for a moment, debating whether or not to say what was on his mind or quit while he was ahead. After a beat, he made up his mind to continue. "Lila, I just want you to know that I intend to rebuild what we once had," he told her. He saw the wary look that came over her face even though he could tell she was trying to appear unaffected by his words. "I didn't say that to scare you, Lila. I want to be fair about this. I'm not going to go behind your back, or spring something on you. This is all going to be aboveboard and honest. I just really want to make the most of this second chance."

"Second chance?" Lila repeated.

The fact that she wasn't immediately dismissing what he'd just said told Everett that at least to some extent, she felt the same way he did. This *was* their second chance. Or more accurately, *his* second chance.

"I think that Fate threw us together like this for a reason, Lila, and I'm not about to ignore that," he told her.

He could see that she still looked wary.

"Don't worry," he reassured her quickly. "I don't plan on throwing a sack over your head and running off with you to some isolated cabin in order to wear you down until you see things my way. I told you that I'm patient and that's not just when it comes to getting a table in a restaurant. I will go as slow as you want me to go, but I have a feeling that in the end, you'll agree with me that we were meant to be together."

As he talked, standing so close to Lila, he was overwhelmed by an urge to kiss her. But he instinctively knew that doing so at this moment would spook her and he couldn't afford the setback that would create. Kissing Lila might satisfy the need he had just to feel her lips against his, but it very well might cost him in the end. He'd be winning the battle but losing the war, so to speak.

So, difficult as it was, he was determined to hold himself in check and wait.

He had no other choice. He had told Lila the truth. Patience was at the very core of his psychological makeup. He intended to wait as long as he had to in order to win Lila back.

"Are you sure that you're up to driving all that distance?" Lila asked him, breaking into his thoughts.

The fact that she worried about him touched Everett again. It proved to him that he was right. In the long run, they were going to wind up together. Fate wouldn't be that cruel to him, to bring her back into his life like this only to ultimately have him lose her a second time. He just had to stay strong and keep his wits about him.

"I'm fine," he told her. "And I'm going to be back sometime next week for a day. I'll see you then," he promised. "Now go inside and lock the door so I can get going."

Lila was about to point out that she got inside her house on her own every night without supervision, or having anything happen to her, but she let it go. She didn't want to ruin the evening. Everett was being protective and there was something to be said for that, she told herself. Besides, being this close to him was practically setting her on fire, which she could not afford.

So she unlocked her door under his watchful eye and then went in, closing the door behind her.

"Now lock it," he told her after a beat, raising his voice to be heard.

"Yes, sir," Lila called back, humoring him. She turned the lock. "It's locked," she announced.

"Good night, Lila."

"Good night, Everett."

And then, after a couple of beats, she heard Everett's car starting up. He was leaving.

Why did that have such a mournful sound to her, she asked herself. After all, she *wanted* him to leave. Everett might be confident about their future together, but she wasn't.

He'd also been confident about their future when they were younger. *Very* confident. And look how that had ultimately turned out, she reminded herself. That big, wonderful future he had been so sure stretched out before them had shriveled up and died before it had ever had a chance to actually take root and thrive.

And history, she reminded herself as she went into her bedroom to change out of her dress, had a terrible habit of repeating itself.

Lila closed her eyes and shivered. She couldn't bear to go though that kind of heartbreak a second time.

She wasn't strong enough.

CHAPTER FOURTEEN

LILA HAD VACILLATED about whether or not to invite Everett to the Fortune Foundation fundraiser for the better part of a week. And now the event was tonight. That meant it was too late for her to change her mind again and invite him.

Just as well, Lila told herself. She'd attend the black-tie gala solo, just as she had initially planned when she'd first gotten the invitation.

Before Everett had popped up back in her life. The only problem was, she felt conflicted.

Ever since Everett had gone out of his way and nursed her through that bout with the flu, she'd been sorely tempted to invite him—just as a show of gratitude, of course. However, she felt that if they attended the function together, that would be like practically announcing to the world at large that they were a couple—again.

And it was much too premature for that sort of speculation to make the rounds.

Because they weren't a couple anymore and they might never *be* a couple.

So, as she wavered back and forth, Lila fell back on her old stand-by: Why borrow trouble?

Consequently, she was going alone.

It wouldn't be the first time, she thought. And given what her life was like, it undoubtedly wouldn't be the last.

The way she felt at the moment, Lila had a premonition that she was destined to be alone for the rest of her life. Her dreams about Everett had been just that: dreams. And sooner or later, people were destined to wake up from dreams.

To boost her spirits, Lila bought herself a brand-new dress. It was a gown really, she thought, looking herself over from all angles in her wardrobe mirror as she prepared to leave.

The floor-length baby-blue silk gown swirled around softly as she moved and made her feel like she was a princess.

A princess without a kingdom—or a prince, Lila added ruefully—but a princess nonetheless.

"At least for one night," Lila whispered to her reflection.

Taking a deep breath, she gathered up her

wrap and her purse. She checked her purse one last time to make sure she had her invitation. It was right where it had been the last four times she'd checked, tucked against her wallet.

She was ready.

"Nothing left to do but drive Cinderella over to the ball," Lila murmured to her reflection.

She smiled to herself as she locked the door and got into her car.

Where are the singing mice when you need them? she wondered wryly, starting up her vehicle.

The Fortune Foundation's fund-raiser was being held on the ground floor ballroom of Austin's finest hotel. Everything about the evening promised to be of the highest, most expensive quality.

After slipping into her purse the ticket that the valet who'd taken her car had given her, Lila went into the hotel.

She didn't need to look at the signs to know which ballroom the fund-raiser was being held in. All she had to do was follow the sound of music and laughter. It was evident that the crowd was having a good time.

The sound quadrupled in volume the second she opened one of the doors to the Golden Room.

She stood there just inside the doors, acclimating herself and looking around what seemed like a cavernous ballroom. There were people absolutely everywhere.

"You made it!"

Surprised, Lila turned to her right and found herself looking at Lucie. Her friend easily hooked her arm through hers.

"I was beginning to think you'd decided to take a pass on this," Lucie said as she began to gently steer Lila in what seemed to be a predetermined direction.

"I didn't think the Foundation allowed us to take a pass," Lila answered honestly. Not that she would have. Her sense of duty and loyalty was just too strong.

"Well, I don't know about 'allowed,'" Lucie replied, considering the matter, "but I do think that there would have been a lot of disappointed people here if you hadn't shown up."

Lila laughed. "I really doubt that," she told Lucie.

"I don't," Lucie retorted. Her eyes were sparkling with humor as she added, "Especially one someone in particular."

Lila stared at her. Lucie had managed to completely lose her. Her brow furrowed as Lila asked, "What are you talking about?"

"Come." The woman tugged a little more insistently on Lila's arm. "I'll show you. By the way, I like the gown. Light blue's a good color for you. It brings out your eyes," she added with approval.

"It's new," Lila confessed, having second thoughts and thinking that maybe she shouldn't have indulged herself like this.

Glancing at the gown one more time, Lucie nodded. "I had a feeling."

"Why? Did I forget to remove a tag?" Lila asked nervously, looking down at her gown and then trying to look over her shoulder to see if there were any telltale tags hanging from the back.

"No, you didn't forget to remove a tag, silly. It just has that first-time-off-a-hanger look." Looking past Lila, Lucie raised her hand and waved.

"Who are you waving at? Chase?" Lila asked, referring to her friend's husband. Scanning the immediate area, Lila tried to get a glimpse of the rancher.

"Chase is off talking to Graham about that pet project of theirs, the center for military equine therapy," Lucie said. She was talking about Graham Fortune, the man who not only had taken over Fortune Cosmetics but also owned the successful Peter's Place, a home where troubled teens were helped to put their lives together. "No," Lucie told her, a very satisfied smile playing on her lips, "I was waving at the person I said would have been disappointed if you'd decided not to attend tonight."

Before Lila could ask any more questions, she suddenly found herself looking up at someone she'd never expected to see.

Everett. In an obligatory tuxedo.

At that moment Lila realized Everett in a tuxedo was even more irresistible than Everett in jeans.

Face it, the man would be irresistible even wearing a kilt.

"What are you doing here?" Lila asked when

she finally located her tongue and remembered how to use it.

"You know, we're going to have to work on getting you a new opening line to say every time you see me," Everett told her with a laugh. "But to answer your question, I was invited."

Lucie stepped up with a slightly more detailed explanation to her friend's question. "The invitation was the Foundation's way of saying thank-you to Everett for his volunteer work."

"Disappointed to see me?" he asked Lila. There was a touch of humor in his voice, although he wasn't quite sure just what to make of the stunned expression on Lila's face.

"No, of course not," Lila denied quickly. "I'm just surprised, that's all. I thought you were still back in Houston."

"I was," Everett confirmed. "The invitation was express-mailed to me yesterday. I thought it would be rude to ignore it, so here I am," he told her simply, as if all he had to do was teleport himself from one location to another instead of drive nearly one hundred and seventy miles.

"Here you are," Lila echoed.

Everything inside her was smiling and she knew that was a dangerous thing. Because when she was in that sort of frame of mind, she tended not to be careful. And that was when mistakes were made.

Mistakes with consequences.

She was going to have to be on her guard, Lila silently warned herself. And it wasn't going to be easy being vigilant, not when Everett looked absolutely, bone-meltingly gorgeous.

As if his dark looks weren't already enough, Lila thought, the tuxedo made Everett look particularly dashing.

You're not eighteen anymore, remember? Lila reminded herself. *You're a woman. A woman who has to be very, very careful.*

She just hoped she could remember that.

"Since your last name practically sounds like Fortune," Lucie was saying to Everett, flanking him on the other side, "maybe you'd like to meet a Fortune or two—or twelve," she teased.

He turned to look at Lila. "Is that all right with you?"

The fact that he asked surprised her. "Why would I object?" she asked, puzzled.

Bending over, he whispered into her ear. "I thought, looking like that," he paused to allow his eyes to skim over her from top to bottom, "maybe you'd want me all to yourself."

She wasn't sure if it was what he said, or his warm breath in her ear that caused the shiver to run rampant up and down her spine.

Whatever it was, it took everything Lila had not to let it get the better of her. She knew where that sort of thing led her. To heaven and then, eventually, to hell as a consequence.

That wasn't going to happen again, she silently swore.

Clearing her throat, Lila ignored the last part of what he'd said and crisply answered, "Yes, it's fine with me."

Lucie smiled. "Then let the introductions begin," she announced, taking charge.

Lucie led off with her husband, Chase. The latter was a genial man who struck Everett as being very down-to-earth, considering the fact that he was an extremely wealthy man.

It was while Everett was talking to Chase that he was introduced to Graham Fortune Robinson. Graham, Everett was told, was one of

Jerome Fortune/Gerald Robinson's eight legitimate offspring. Again, rather than behaving as if he was spoiled or indifferent, or extremely entitled—all traits that Everett had seen displayed by many of the wealthy people he'd grown up with—Graham Fortune came across as only interested in the amount of good he could do with the money he had.

The man, like so many of the other Fortunes who were there that evening, had a keen interest in philanthropy, Everett concluded.

While he was being introduced to and talking with various members of the Fortune clan, Everett found himself exploring the subject that was so near and dear to Schuyler's heart: that perhaps there was some sort of a family connection between the Fortune family and his own. Was "Fortunado" just a poor attempt by someone in the previous generation to either connect to the Fortunes, or to clumsily try to hide that connection?

Everett's radar went up even higher when, after Lucie said that her connection to Graham went beyond just bloodlines, Graham joked that it seemed like everyone was related to him these days.

Everett forced himself to bite his tongue in order to refrain from asking Graham if, by that comment, he was referring to the Fortunados.

The next moment, Graham cleared up the possible confusion by saying that he was referring to the fact that numerous illegitimate Fortune offspring had been located over the past couple of years. Apparently, many years ago the prodigious patriarch Jerome Fortune had deliberately disappeared. When he had resurfaced, he had changed his name, calling himself Gerald Robinson. And, in addition to going on to amass a wealthy portfolio of his own, Gerald/Jerome had amassed a sizeable number of offspring, both legitimately with his wife, Charlotte, and illegitimately with a whole host of women whose paths the man had crossed.

"How did he manage to keep track of all those kids?" Everett marveled, still trying to wrap his mind around the fact that one man had wound up fathering a legion of children.

"Quite simply, he didn't," Graham answered. "But according to one story I've heard, his wife—and my mother—did. She got it into her head to look up every one of her husband's progeny. Some of my siblings think she wanted to be prepared for any eventuality," Graham explained. "Supposedly, she has everything she found written down in a big binder or something along those lines."

Graham smiled. "My personal theory is that when she collected enough data to make that binder really heavy, she was going to use it to hit my father upside the head and teach him a lesson for tomcatting around like that."

Lila nodded, saying in all seriousness, "If you ask me, the man certainly had it coming, spreading his seed around like that without any thought of how this was affecting anyone else in his family—especially those children."

"Yes, but then on the other hand, if he hadn't done it, there would be a lot less Fortunes in the world and so far, all the ones I've met have been really decent people whose hearts are in the right place," Everett pointed out.

Graham smiled his approval at Everett's comment. "I couldn't have put it better myself. I've come to like every one of my siblings." He shrugged and held up his wineglass as if in a silent toast to them. "It's not everyone who has a family big enough to populate a medium-size town."

Everett touched his glass to Graham's. He felt as if he could go on talking about the various members of the Fortune family all night. But suddenly, everyone in the ballroom was being asked to stop what they were doing.

"Can I have everyone's attention for a moment?" a tall, imposing man with a booming voice said into a microphone. He was standing before a podium at the front of the ballroom. "This is the time in our evening where we all temporarily suspend the festivities and are asked to dig deep into our hearts—and our pockets," the MC added with a laugh. "In other words, it's time for us to donate to the Fortune Foundation so it can go on doing all those good works and helping all those people who are not nearly as fortunate—no pun intended—as we all are."

The man's piercing blue eyes seemed to sweep around the entire ballroom. No easy feat, Lila thought, watching from the sidelines.

"Now don't be shy," the MC continued. "Give

as much as you're able. No donation is too small, although bigger is always better. But even a little is better than nothing. So, like I said, open your hearts and get those checkbooks out. Remember, it feels good to give. And when you do, you'll find that you'll get back in ways you never even suspected were possible."

Listening, Lila opened up her purse and took out her checkbook. She was about to start writing out what she viewed to be a modest amount—although it was all she could afford—when Everett put his hand on hers, stopping her.

She looked at him, puzzled. Why wasn't he letting her write the check?

"I'll take care of it for both of us," he told her. The next moment, as she watched, she saw Everett write out a check for the sum of one hundred thousand dollars.

At the last second, she remembered to keep her mouth from dropping open.

CHAPTER FIFTEEN

THE MC, DAVID DAVENPORT, looked at the check that had just been passed to him by one of the aides collecting donations from the guests. Holding the check aloft, Davenport scanned the crowd until he made eye contact with Everett.

"Is this right?" the MC asked Everett, astonished. "Your pen didn't slip?"

Everett's mouth curved slightly as he smiled at the man in front of the room. "My pen didn't slip," he assured the MC.

Davenport, a distinguished-looking, gray-haired man in his fifties, instantly brightened. "Ladies and gentlemen, I'm proud to announce that we have a new record," he told the gathering. "Dr. Everett Fortunado has generously donated the sum of one hundred thousand dollars to the Fortune Foundation."

A hush fell over the entire ballroom. It lasted for almost a full minute and then people began clapping. The sound swelled until the entire ballroom was engulfed in appreciative applause.

Everett wasn't really sure just how to react to the applause. He hadn't made the donation because he wanted to garner any sort of attention. He'd written the check because he felt it was his obligation to share the good fortune he had always felt so privileged to grow up experiencing.

When the applause finally died down, Davenport proceeded to try to utilize the moment to the Foundation's advantage.

"All right, people, let's see if Dr. Fortunado's generosity can motivate some of you to do your fair share as well." The MC looked around. It seemed as if he was making eye contact with everyone there. "Remember, this is for those deserving mothers and fathers and children who so badly need our help in order to make it through the hard times."

Everett stood back and watched as more of the fund-raiser's attendees began writing out checks. There seemed to be chatter going on all around him.

Except at his side.

From the moment he had written out the check, Everett noticed that Lila had fallen completely silent. She hadn't said a single word to him during the entire time that the checks were being written and collected on all sides of them.

Nor, he observed, did Lila say anything during the buffet dinner that followed, despite the fact that he had intentionally stayed close to her during the whole time. He had broached a number of topics in an effort to engage her in conversation and had only received single-word replies.

Finally, unable to take the silence any longer, he drew Lila aside to a little alcove, away from the rest of the ballroom, and asked her point-blank: "Is something wrong?"

Lila had been trying to reconcile the mixed feelings she'd been having ever since she'd watched Everett writing out a check for such an exorbitant amount. Because she didn't want to cause a scene or start an uproar, she'd been doing her best just to squelch the suspicions that had been growing in her head. That involved keeping her mouth shut and not saying anything, although it wasn't easy.

But her doubts weren't going away, and rather than taking a hint and keeping quiet, Everett was pressuring her for an explanation.

Finally blowing out a frustrated breath, Lila asked him bluntly, "Are you trying to buy me?"

Dumbfounded and more than a little confused, Everett could only stare at her. He wasn't even sure if he had actually heard Lila correctly.

"What?"

Lila pressed her lips together, then ground out, "Are you trying to buy my love by giving that huge sum of money to the Foundation?"

Stunned, he told her, "I made that donation because the Foundation is a worthy cause that does a great deal of good work. I thought you'd be happy about my contribution." He looked at her, not knowing where this had come from. Not for the first time, he felt as if he was walking on eggshells around her.

"Why do you have to dissect every single move I make and search for an ulterior motive?" he wanted to know. "Can't I just be generous because I want to be? Because it makes me feel good to do something decent for people who weren't born as lucky as I was?" He saw tears suddenly shimmering in her eyes and immediately felt a pang of guilt because he knew he was responsible for those tears. "Hey, I didn't mean to make you cry—"

Lila shook her head, halting his apology. Taking a deep breath to center herself, she said, "You didn't. You're right. You did something selfless and I just took it apart, looking for hidden reasons behind your donation when you were just being a decent guy." She blew out a shaky breath. "I guess I've just gotten to be really mistrustful."

And that was on him, Everett thought. He'd done this to her—taken a sweet, optimistic young woman and crushed something inside of her all those years ago. He had to find a way to fix this, he told himself.

But how?

How did he convince Lila that his feelings for her were genuine? That all he wanted was to be able to show her that he loved her and that he was willing to make things up to her for the rest of his life?

Desperation had him making the next move in his desire to reach her, to communicate to her just how sincere he was.

Since he had taken her away from the rest of the guests in the ballroom by drawing her into a recessed alcove to talk to her, he knew they'd be safe from any prying eyes.

Framing Lila's face with his hands, Everett bent his head and did what he had been longing to do since he had first seen her in that sandwich shop in Austin.

He kissed her.

The moment his lips touched Lila's, Everett realized just how much he had missed her.

How much he really wanted Lila.

A little voice in his head told him he should stop kissing her, but he couldn't. Instead, Everett deepened the kiss.

And just like that, the captor became the captive.

At that moment, he knew that he would have walked through fire just to have Lila back in his life the way she had been all those years ago: loving and untainted by uncertainties and doubts.

Lila's breath caught in her throat. A split second before Everett had kissed her, she suddenly knew that he would. Knew too that with all her heart she wanted him to kiss her.

And then he did.

Just like that, all those years they'd spent apart melted away. She was instantly responding to Everett just as she had back then.

Except that now Lila was responding as a woman, not as a starry-eyed young girl.

Lila could feel every inch of her body heating as she fell deeper into the kiss. She wrapped her arms around Everett, savoring the taste of his lips urgently pressed against hers.

Longings, locked away for so long, came charging out, demanding attention as they carelessly trampled reason into the dust.

Her heart was pounding wildly when he drew his lips away. She found herself struggling in order to pull air into her lungs.

She looked up at Everett in wonder, desire mounting within her.

He hadn't meant to get this carried away, to let the moment get out of hand like this. He'd only wanted to kiss Lila again, to silently communicate to her that his feelings for her were as strong as ever.

Stronger.

"I'm sorry, Lila," Everett began. "I didn't mean to get—"

But Lila quickly cut short his apology. She didn't want Everett to be sorry for kissing her. Didn't want to have him withdrawing from her. Not when she was suddenly having all these unresolved feelings ricocheting throughout every inch of her being.

She wanted more.

Needed more.

"Let's get out of here," Lila breathed.

She didn't mean that, Everett thought, even as he asked, "Now?"

"Now," she echoed adamantly.

Everett stood there for a moment arguing with himself, trying very hard to convince himself to do the right thing.

Another man would have talked her out of it, pointing out what it might look like if someone saw them leaving before the fund-raiser was over. Another man would have taken her by the hand and led her back into the ballroom proper.

But another man hadn't spent every day of the last thirteen years missing Lila so much that there were times he literally ached.

Now that there was a glimmer of hope that they could get back together, that he could win her back, he could admit that to himself. Admit that the reason that every possible relationship that had loomed before him over the years had fallen through was because all the women in those would-be relationships hadn't been able to hold a candle to Lila.

So instead of doing the noble thing and trying to talk Lila out of what she'd just suggested, Everett took her hand in his. And together they made their way out of the ballroom. And then out of the hotel.

Once outside, as the cooler evening air slipped over them, Everett looked at Lila for some sign that she'd had a change of heart about leaving. He didn't detect any, but because he absolutely wanted her to have no regrets, he asked, "You're sure?"

"I'm sure," Lila answered breathlessly. All she wanted was to be alone with him. To be with him in every way possible.

"We both drove here separately," Everett reminded her.

While he feared that if she drove herself she might change her mind, he knew that if Lila left her car here at the hotel, someone from the fund-raiser would take note of that.

Questions would be asked and gossip would spread. He didn't want Lila subjected to any sort of talk or speculation as to why her car was still in the parking structure while she herself was nowhere to be found. He wanted to protect her from that sort of thing at all costs.

Although she didn't want to be more than a foot away from him right now, Lila didn't see any actual problem. "So? We can both drive our cars to my house. My driveway can accommodate two vehicles," she told him.

Lila could feel her heart hammering with every word she uttered as a tiny voice in her head, barely audible above the beating of her heart, was telling her to take her car and make good her escape.

But she didn't want to escape. One taste of Everett's lips and it was all she could do not to beg for more right here, right now.

When the valet came up to them, they both handed him their tickets.

"Bring the lady her car first," Everett told him.

The valet nodded. "Be right back," he promised, heading into the parking structure quickly.

"Think anyone noticed you left?" Everett asked her as they waited.

"If they notice anyone's gone, it would most likely be you," Lila told him. "After all, you're the man of the hour after that huge donation."

When the valet brought her car up and held the door open for her, she handed him a tip and then slid into the driver's seat.

She looked up at Everett, said, "I'll see you," and then drove off.

I'll see you.

Her words echoed in his brain. She hadn't said "I'll see you *later.*" Just "I'll see you." Did that mean she'd had a change of heart and decided that she'd almost made a terrible mistake?

Now who's overthinking everything? Everett admonished himself.

He put the original question on hold when the valet brought up his car.

"You car handles like a dream," the valet told him enthusiastically and a bit enviously as he got out of the vehicle. Backing away, he left the driver's door open for him.

Everett inclined his head, a grin curving his mouth. "She likes to be babied," he told the valet as he handed him a ten-dollar bill and got in.

The valet's eyes widened as he looked at the bill. "Thanks!"

Everett pulled away, eager to catch up to Lila's car. But it felt like he was catching every single red light between the hotel and her house.

He really hoped that by the time he got there Lila hadn't reflected on her impulsive decision and changed her mind about the night ahead.

If she did, he would have no choice but to go along with her decision. He would never force himself on her, but he decided that he was going to do everything in his power to convince her that they were meant to be together.

Because they were.

It was hard to stay focused on the road. All he could see in his mind's eye was Lila. Lila, offering herself to him. Lila, making love with him.

Lila, who was and always had been the center of his universe.

How had he allowed himself to let her go? Everett silently asked himself. He wouldn't have tied her up in the attic, but he could have tried to talk her out of breaking up with him, could have tried his damnedest to convince her to give him another chance.

Well, this is your chance, Everett, he thought as he turned onto Lila's block. *Don't blow it.*

CHAPTER SIXTEEN

WHAT IF EVERETT didn't come?

What if he did?

Lila pressed her hand against her stomach, trying to quiet the butterflies that seemed to be wildly crashing into one another in her stomach. She'd never felt so confused before.

Back in the ballroom alcove, when Everett had kissed her, awakening all those old feelings, she'd wanted him right then and there. But now she'd had a little time to distance herself from that kiss, doubts had begun creeping in. It was as if she was playing a tennis match with herself in her brain.

Where *was* he?

Granted she'd flown through every light and gotten home in record time, moving as if her car was being propelled by a gale, but she hadn't left *that* much ahead of Everett.

He should have been here by now.

Unless he'd changed his mind and decided to go straight to his sister's house instead.

Or maybe he'd just decided to head back to Houston from the fund-raiser instead of coming over to her house.

To her.

Had she come on too strong?

But after he kissed her like that, unearthing all those old memories, she just couldn't help herself. Any thoughts of hanging back or taking it slow had just incinerated right on the spot. All she could think of was how much she'd missed being in Everett's arms, of having him hold her as if she was something very precious.

She felt as if she was losing her mind.

Lila looked out her window and saw only her car in the driveway.

He'd had a change of heart, she thought, letting the curtain drop back into place.

With a gut-wrenching sigh, she turned away. Served her right for giving in to her emotions like some silly schoolgirl and—

She jerked her head up, listening. Was that—?

Yes, it was. It was the sound of a car pulling up in her driveway.

All those doubts that were surfacing took a nosedive and she threw open the door before he had a chance to ring the doorbell.

"There are way too many red lights in this city," Everett told her.

Grabbing hold of his shirt, Lila pulled him over the threshold and into her house, slamming the door shut right behind him.

"I don't want to talk about red lights," she said just before she rose up on her tiptoes and sealed her mouth to his.

It was more than a couple of minutes later that they managed to come up for air—temporarily.

"Right," Everett breathlessly agreed, devouring her with his eyes. "No talking about red lights."

"No talking at all," Lila countered.

As she sought out his lips again, sealing hers to them, she began to systematically remove Everett's tuxedo, separating it from his body so quickly she worried that she'd wind up ripping something.

If she did, she could fix it, she assured herself. She knew her way around a needle. But right now, she wanted to relearn her way around his body.

It had been a long, long time since she'd been intimate with him. Since she'd been intimate with *anyone*, because after she had left Everett, she'd never met anyone to take his place, or even come close to qualifying as a candidate for that position. Without love as an ingredient in the mix, lovemaking just didn't seem right to her.

As she was eagerly removing his clothing, Everett was doing the same with hers.

Lila could feel his hands moving along her body. Locating her zipper, he pulled it down her back in one swift movement, then peeled away the silky gown from her skin.

It fell to the floor like a sinking blue cloud, pooling about her high heels.

Lila caught her breath as she felt his strong hands tugging away her bikini underwear, then gliding over her bare skin, swiftly reducing her to a pulsating mass of desire.

With urgent movements, she hurried to return the compliment until they were both standing there in her living room, nude—except for one thing.

She was still wearing her high heels.

Lila quickly remedied that, kicking the shoes off and instantly becoming petite.

"Damn," Everett whispered against the sensitive skin of her throat as he pressed kiss after kiss along it, "I can't tell you how many times I've dreamed about doing this."

The feel of his warm breath sliding along her skin caused all her desires to intensify. Her mushrooming needs almost engulfed her as they seized control over every single facet of her being.

Her mind in a haze, Lila felt her back being pressed against the sofa. She didn't even remember how they got there.

Everett was taking inventory of every single inch of her body with his mouth, creating wonderful sensations as he moved.

Doing wonderful things.

She was eager to return the favor, but for the moment, she couldn't find the strength to do anything but absorb every nuance of what was happening. She was utterly immersed in the deliciously wicked feelings that were erupting all over her as his lips and tongue left their mark everywhere, branding her.

Making her his.

Lila twisted and arched, savoring and absorbing every wondrous salvo wildly echoing throughout her body.

And still he continued, moving lower and lower by pulsating increments.

Anticipation rippled through her like shockwaves as she felt first his breath, and then his mouth moving down to the very center of her core.

His tongue teased her ever so lightly, skimming along the delicate, sensitive area, all the while raising her response higher and higher, creating a fever pitch within her until finally, delicious explosions erupted simultaneously all through her, undulating over her like a series of earthquakes.

Lila cried out his name, pulling him to her until he was right above her, melting her soul with the intense look of desire and passion in his eyes.

She felt him coaxing open her legs with his

knee. What there was left of her shallow breath caught in her throat.

The next moment, he entered her and they were sealed to one another, creating a single heated entity.

Everett began to move his hips so slowly at first, she thought she had only imagined it. But then the movements began to increase, growing stronger. Taking her with them.

And then they were no longer on her sofa, no longer in her house. They were somewhere else, completely isolated from the world. A place where only the two of them existed.

The only thing that mattered was Everett and this insanely wondrous sensation that they were sharing. Their bodies danced to music that only the two of them could hear.

The tempo increased, going faster and faster until suddenly they found themselves racing to the top of the world, to a place that was both new and familiar at the same time.

Lila could feel her heart slamming against his. Could feel Everett's heart echoing hers to the point that she thought their two hearts would forever be sealed together as one.

And then she felt the fireworks exploding, showering a profusion of stars all around her until that was all there was.

A world filed with stars.

She clung to Everett then, clung to the sensation that they had created together. She clung to it for as long as she could and bathed in the euphoria that came in its wake.

She held onto the sensation—and Everett—for as long as possible. But even so, it receded no matter how hard she fought to hang onto it.

Sorrow began to wiggle its way into the spaces the euphoria had left behind.

Everett shifted his weight off her, moving so that he was lying beside her.

He tightened his arm around her, exulting in the feeling of warmth generated by holding onto her. He glanced down at his chest and was mildly surprised that he wasn't glowing or giving out some sort of light like a beacon that guided the ships through the night at sea.

She was back, he thought. He'd won Lila back. And the lovemaking between them was so much better now than it had been before.

The sex might have been familiar at its roots, but it had also felt wonderfully brand-new.

The woman in his arms was so much more now than she had been all those years ago.

How did he get so lucky? Everett silently marveled. Lying here next to Lila, reliving the lovemaking they had just shared, he found himself wanting to take her all over again.

Wanting her with a renewed fierceness that was impossible to ignore.

Propping himself up slightly, Everett leaned over her face and kissed one eyelid, then her other eyelid.

Then her mouth.

He lingered there, deepening the kiss until it all but consumed both of them, feeding something in his soul.

And then hers.

She looked up at him with wonder. "Again?" she questioned.

Lila saw laughter entering his eyes as Everett told her, "Honey, I am just getting started."

Something came over her.

Lila seized the moment and just like that, turned the tables on him. It was her turn to be the seducer rather than the seduced. This relationship didn't have a prayer of working if only one of them gave while the other received, she thought.

So, just as he had done before, Lila began to prime his body, ever so lightly gliding both her lips and her tongue along all the sensitive, seducible areas of his body.

Priming him until he verged on the edge of full readiness.

She moved with purpose along Everett's chest, gliding the tip of her tongue along his nipples just as he had done to her.

And then she slid her tongue along the hard contours of his chest, moving steadily down to his belly, teasing it until it quivered beneath her hot, probing mouth.

Raising her eyes, she met his. A wicked look entered them as she proceeded to work her way lower along his anatomy until she had reached his hardening desire.

With an air of triumph, she went on to make him hers by branding him.

She did it, once, then twice—then suddenly, she felt his hands on her forearms, stopping her.

He drew her away and brought her back up to his level by pulling her body along his.

Arousing both of them even more.

The next second, he raised his head and captured her mouth with his own, kissing her over and over again until he had reduced her to the consistency of a rain puddle that was about to go up in the steam of a hot summer sun. At that moment, he deftly switched their places. He was above her and she was back under him.

And just as before, they united, forming one whole.

This time he moved urgently right from the start. There was no gentle increase in tempo. There were just the swift, direct movements that were intended to bring them swirling up to journey's end.

And it did.

So quickly that it stole away their breath, leaving them gasping and panting in the aftermath of the crescendo that had brought all the stars raining down on them.

As before, the euphoria that sealed around them in the aftermath was wondrous. And, also as before, it slipped away much too soon, leaving Lila exhausted and slowly making her way back to reality.

With painstakingly slow movements, Lila shifted her head so that she was looking at the man next to her without alerting him to the fact that she was.

It was happening. Happening just as she had been afraid that it would.

She could feel it.

She was falling in love with Everett all over again. And she was totally powerless to prevent it, she thought with a sliver of panic that was beginning to grow inside of her.

Why had she done this?

Why had she allowed it to happen? She could have stopped it from ever taking place—*should* have stopped it from taking place not once, but twice, she ruefully reminded herself. She had allowed the evening—and herself—to spin completely out of control and now she had consequences to face.

She didn't like this feeling, this feeling of being unable to stop her life from spinning out of control.

Lila could feel herself growing more and

more afraid. Afraid of what she'd done. Afraid of where she just *knew* it was going to lead—to the same unhappiness she'd experienced thirteen years ago.

How could something that had felt so right in the moment be so very wrong in the long run?

But it was, she thought.

It was.

What made her think that just because they'd managed to recapture the rapturous happiness of lovemaking it was destined to end any other way for them than it already had once before?

Those that do not learn from history are doomed to repeat it.

And that was her, she thought ruefully. She was doomed to repeat the mistakes she'd made once. In fact, she already had repeated those mistakes.

Well, she *could* learn from her mistakes, Lila silently insisted. And she intended to start right now, before it was too late and things spun further out of control, setting the stage for Everett to break her heart all over again.

Summoning her resolve, not to mention her

courage, Lila turned toward the man lying next to her on the sectional sofa.

She struggled into an upright position.

Everett shift toward her. "Want to take this to your bedroom and do it again?" he asked her with a warm, inviting smile.

"No," she said with such finality that it froze Everett in place. "I want you to leave."

The blissful happiness he'd just been experiencing broke up into tiny slivered shards. He felt as if he'd just been blindsided.

Everett stared at her. "Did I do something wrong?" he asked, trying to understand why she had made this unexpected U-turn.

"Things are moving too fast, Everett," she told him. Her tone left no room for any sort of attempts to change her mind. "You need to go."

CHAPTER SEVENTEEN

EVERETT SAT UP. "You're really serious?" he asked, unable to believe that Lila actually meant what she'd just said to him.

He'd been with a number of women since he and Lila had broken up and although he'd never gotten to the serious relationship stage with any of those women, none of them had ever kicked him out of bed, either, figuratively *or* literally.

His confidence shaken, Everett had no idea how to react to this totally unfamiliar situation.

Lila had already gotten up off the sofa, wrapping a crocheted throw around herself in lieu of clothing. Her insides were quaking, but she held her ground.

"Yes, I'm serious," she insisted, her voice rising in pitch. "*Very* serious."

Well, he'd tried his best and for a little while there, he thought that he'd succeeded in winning Lila over. But obviously, he'd miscalculated, Everett told himself. He was willing to do anything to win Lila back except for one thing: he was not about to beg. A man had to have some pride, he thought fiercely.

Nodding his head, he quickly pulled on his discarded tuxedo slacks. Securing them, he grabbed the rest of his things and held the clothes against his chest in a rumpled ball of material. He didn't even bother putting on his shoes. Instead, he just picked them up and held them in his other hand.

"All right then," he told her, heading for the door. "I'd better go."

Lila stood like a statue, saying nothing.

Everett let himself out the door, leaving it wide open. As he walked to his car in the driveway, he heard the front door close with finality behind him, obliterating any hope that at the last minute Lila would change her mind and either come running after him or at least call him back into the house.

Forcing himself not to look back, Everett opened his car door and got into his vehicle. He felt so totally stunned and deflated that he could hardly breathe as he started up his car and pulled out of Lila's driveway.

He stopped at the first all-night gas station he came to. Ignoring the convenience store clerk's curious looks, he asked for the restroom key. Taking it from the man, he let himself into the single stall bathroom.

The conditions in the restroom were far from ideal, but he managed to put on the rest of his clothes. He wanted to avoid having Schuyler ask him a barrage of questions if he walked in wearing only the tuxedo slacks.

He loved his sister dearly, but he just wasn't up to fielding any of her questions, however well intentioned they might be. He just wanted to quietly get his things from her guest room and drive back to Houston.

But as luck would have it, a swift, clean getaway was just not in the cards for him.

Despite the hour, Schuyler was up and heard him coming in. Everett had barely closed the front door and walked in before his sister walked out of the kitchen and managed to waylay him at the foot of the stairs.

"What are you doing back so soon?" she

asked him in surprise. "I wasn't expecting you back until around midmorning."

He offered her a careless shrug in response. "Fund-raiser ended so I came back."

Schuyler furrowed her brow, as if something didn't sound right to her. "Why didn't you go get a nightcap with Lila?"

"I didn't want to drink and drive," Everett answered. He looked longingly up the stairs. So near and yet so far, he couldn't help thinking.

Schuyler's furrowed brow gave way to an all-out, impatient frown.

"Damn it, Ev, I'm trying to politely tiptoe around the subject but you're making me have to come flat out and ask." She paused, waiting for her brother to jump in and say what she was waiting for him to tell her. But he remained silent. Huffing, Schuyler asked, "Why aren't you over at Lila's place, picking things up where the two of you left off back in college?"

"It's complicated, Schuy," Everett told her.

"That's what people say when they don't want to deal with something," she insisted. She pinned her brother with a penetrating look that went clear down to the bone. "Do you care about this woman?" she asked him point-blank.

Still smarting from his rejection, he *really* didn't want to get into this with his sister. "Schuyler, go to bed."

They had always talked things out before and Schuyler apparently refused to back off now that she had broached the subject. "Do you care about this woman?" she repeated, enunciating each word slowly with intentional emphasis.

He could see that Schuyler wasn't about to let this go until she had an answer from him. So he gave her one. A short one.

"No."

Schuyler's eyes narrowed, looking deep into his. "You're lying."

Everett did his best to separate himself from any emotion. He really didn't want to shout at his sister. "No, I'm not."

"Yes, you are," Schuyler retorted. When he tried to turn away, she grabbed hold of his shoulder, making him face her. "You have this 'tell' when you lie. There's a tiny nerve right under your left eye that jumps every time you don't tell the truth."

"Then why even bother asking me?" He came close to biting off his question.

"So you can hear the words out loud for yourself," she told him. "Ev, when you first told me you were going to win Lila back, I didn't think you had a chance in hell of doing it. I thought you'd eventually come to your senses and forget the whole thing."

She shook her head, amused by her preconceived notion. "But you're not the type to forget the whole thing and you managed to bring me around to your way of thinking. A guy like that doesn't just give up out of the blue."

Taking his hand, Schuyler tugged on it, making him sit down on the bottom step. She sat down beside him, just the way they used to do as kids whenever they wanted to talk about things.

"What happened?" she asked him.

After a short internal debate, Everett gave her an abbreviated version, mentioning his donation to the Foundation in passing, but not the amount.

He told his sister about going back with Lila to her place, but left it for her imagination to fill in the details of what transpired there. He ended by telling his sister that Lila had suddenly pulled back, saying that things were going too fast and that he needed to go home.

"And...?" Schuyler asked, waiting for him to tell her more.

"And I came home," Everett said with a shrug. "Or to your house," he corrected. "I wanted to change out of this monkey suit, get my suitcase and go back to Houston."

"And nothing else happened?" she questioned, studying his face closely.

"Nothing else happened," he echoed flatly. He just wanted to get his things and hit the road, putting this night—and Lila—behind him.

Schuyler's mouth curved in a tolerant, loving smile. "You do realize that your shirt is inside out, don't you?" his sister asked. "Did you wear it that way at the fund-raiser?"

He glanced down. Damn it, leave it to Schuyler to catch that, he thought, annoyed. "Yup. The whole fund-raiser," he told her stubbornly.

"I see," Schuyler replied, watching the nerve just beneath his eye flutter. "Well, maybe nobody noticed," she said loftily. "Or maybe Lila did and that's why she told you things were moving too fast and sent you away." Schuyler's smile widened. "She didn't want to be associated with someone who couldn't dress himself properly."

"Schuyler—" There was a warning note in Everett's voice.

Schuyler held up her hands, warding off what he was about to say.

"I'm just teasing you," she told him. And then her tone changed. "Why don't you stay here for what's left of the night and then go talk to Lila in the morning?" she suggested. "Things always look better in the morning," she added kindly.

"No," he told his sister, his mind made up. "I need to be getting back. I've let a lot of things slide lately and I need to do some catching up."

"That's not the Dr. Everett Fortunado I know," Schuyler told him, rising to her feet when he did. "You can juggle more balls in the air than any two people I know."

"Not this time," he answered as he started up the steps. "This time those balls are all falling right through my hands."

"Want me to help you pack?" she offered, calling up the stairs.

"No, I've got this," he told her, glancing over his shoulder.

Schuyler stood there, arms akimbo, and murmured loud enough for him to hear, "No, I don't think that you do."

"That was some hefty donation that your boyfriend made on Friday," Lucie said the following Monday morning as Lila passed her open door.

Lila made no answer, merely shrugging in response as she stepped into her office.

Lucie didn't take the hint. Instead, she followed her friend into Lila's office. When Lila sat down at her desk, Lucie peered at her a little more closely.

"You look awful," she observed. Then a small smile lit her eyes. "Didn't get any sleep all weekend, huh?"

"No," Lila answered, deliberately not taking Lucie's bait. Her tone flatly denied any further dialogue between them.

But Lucie wasn't about to take the hint. "So how was it?" she asked with a grin.

Lila spared her friend a glance. Lucie was now firmly planted on the edge of her desk. "How was what?"

"You know..." But since Lila gave no indication that she did, Lucie further elaborated. "Getting back together with Everett."

"We're not back together," Lila answered, biting off each word. They all had a bitter taste, but that would pass, she told herself. It *had* to.

"Why the hell not?" Lucie cried. When Lila looked at her sharply, Lucie said, "Anyone at the fund-raiser could see he was crazy about you. When you two left early, I was sure you were going back to your place—if you made it that far," Lucie added.

This time Lila's head shot up. She was really hoping that no one had noticed them leaving the fund-raiser. So much for hoping.

"What's that supposed to mean?" she wanted to know.

Lucie sighed.

"Lila, there were so many sparks flying between the two of you that you'd make an electrical storm seem like an afternoon at the library in comparison." She gave Lila a deep, penetrating look, as if willing the truth out of her. "You can't tell me that you two didn't get together after you left the fund-raiser."

"All right," Lila replied grudgingly. It wasn't in her to lie. "We did."

Getting up off the desk, Lucie closed Lila's door, then crossed back to her desk, coming closer. "And?" she coaxed.

Lila shifted uncomfortably in her chair, but it was clear that Lucie wasn't going anywhere until she heard all the details.

"And then I sent him away," she said, jumping to the end without elaborating anything in between.

Lucie stared at her. "You're joking."

"No, I'm not," Lila replied firmly. "I sent him away."

"Why in heaven's name would you do that?" Lucie cried incredulously.

"Because things were moving much too fast between us," Lila blurted out, frustration bubbling beneath her statement.

Leaning forward, Lucie took her friend's

hands into hers. "Lila, honey," she began gently, "it's been thirteen years. After all that time, things were not moving fast. They were barely crawling by at a turtle's pace." She squeezed Lila's hands as she looked deeper into her eyes, as if trying to understand, to read Lila's thoughts. And then it must have hit her, because she sharply drew a breath. "You got scared, didn't you? He made you have all those feelings again and it scared you."

Lila looked away. Lucie had homed in on the truth.

But there was no running from the truth. She knew that now.

With a sigh, she nodded. And then she looked up at Lucie. "How did you do it?" she asked, silently begging the other woman for guidance.

"Do what?" Lucie asked.

"With Chase," Lila said, hoping that Lucie had some sage, magical knowledge to impart. Some words of wisdom that could somehow guide her through this densely wooded area she found herself stumbling through. "How were you able to pick up where you left off with Chase?" The two hadn't just been high school sweethearts, they'd eloped and had been married—for all of five minutes.

"Very easy," Lucie answered her nonchalantly. "I didn't."

Lila stared at her. She didn't understand. "But you two were just recently married."

"Actually, we'd been secretly married as teenagers and never had it annulled, but didn't find out until recently. We had to get to know each other as adults, not as the impulsive kids we once were. And that's what you have to do," Lucie told her in all honesty. "You and Everett have to do the work and get to know each other all over again—from scratch," she insisted. "You have to take into consideration that Everett, in all likelihood, may very well *not* be the person he was at sixteen or eighteen or twenty."

Lucie circled to the back of the desk and put her arm on Lila's shoulder.

"And while we're at it, why do you assume that history has to repeat itself?" she questioned gently. "What if Everett really means what he says and wants to get back together with you not for a romp or a weekend of love-making, but for good?"

Lila rose from her chair and paced about the small office. She couldn't come to grips with the desperate feeling she was experiencing in her gut.

"Even if Everett's serious, even if he wants things to be different this time around, the past is still standing between us like a giant road-block," Lila insisted.

"By the past you mean the little girl that you gave up." It wasn't a question. Lucie was reading between the lines. She knew the truth about Lila's past. In a moment of weakness, Lila had entrusted her with her deepest secret.

"Yes," Lila cried, struggling not to cry. "It still haunts me," she admitted. "Holding her in my arms and then giving her up—some nights I still wake up in a cold sweat, remembering how that felt. To have her and then not have her, all in the blink of an eye," Lila confessed sadly.

"Does Everett realize how you feel?" Lucie asked.

Lila pressed her lips together and shook her

head. "I don't know," she answered. "I never said anything about it."

"Did you *ask* him if he knew?" Lucie pressed. "Or say anything at all about what giving her up did to you?"

"No," Lila admitted in a low voice, avoiding Lucie's eyes.

"Then for heaven sakes, *talk* to him about it," Lucie urged. "Tell him how you felt giving up your baby. How you *still* feel."

"I can't," Lila said. "I just can't. Lucie, I know you mean well, but just please, please leave me alone right now. It'll work out."

It will, Lila told herself as Lucie walked out of her office.

It had to.

CHAPTER EIGHTEEN

"ALL RIGHT, I'M HERE," Everett declared when his sister opened her front door to admit him into her house several days later. "I got Blake to take over a few of my patients, had the rest of them rescheduled and drove right out because you sounded as if this was urgent." His eyes swept over her and she certainly didn't look as if she was in the throes of some sort of an emergency. "Now what's this all about?"

Instead of answering his question, Schuyler said, "I can't tell you here." Getting her purse, she took out her car keys. "In order to explain, I need to take you some place first."

Everett looked at his sister suspiciously. This wasn't making any sense to him. "Where?" he wanted to know.

Again she avoided giving him a direct answer. "You'll understand everything once we're there," Schuyler told him, hurrying toward her spacious garage.

Fetching her red BMW, she pulled up next to her brother. "Get in," she told him, leaning over and throwing open the passenger door.

Since he'd all but raced out of Houston, driving at top speed until he'd reached Austin because he was extremely concerned about Schuyler, he went along with her instructions.

"You're being awfully mysterious about all this," he accused.

"The mystery will be cleared up before you know it, big brother," Schuyler promised, mentally crossing her fingers.

Everett suddenly sat up a little straighter in the passenger seat as a thought occurred to him.

Looking at her now, he asked, "Hey, Schuy, you're not pregnant, are you?" As the question came out of his mouth, he began grinning so widely, his lips almost hurt. He'd thought his sister would get married first before starting a family, but that didn't negate his happiness for her. "Wow, that's terrific. How far along are you?" he asked excitedly. "What does Carlo think about this? Have you picked a godfather yet?"

Apparently overwhelmed, Schuyler took a second to speak. "Hey, slow down," she said then. She slanted a look in his direction before turning back to the road. "So you like the idea of babies," she said, obviously referring to his exuberant reaction.

"Of course I do. How far along are you?" he asked her again.

"I'm not," Schuyler told him.

Everett looked as if his bubble had been pierced, sending him twisting in the wind. "Wait, I don't understand. Then you're not pregnant?" he asked, more confused than ever.

"No," Schuyler answered. "I never said I was. *You* jumped to that conclusion," she pointed out. "Let me have my wedding first, then we'll see about babies."

Everett slumped back against his seat. "Okay, then I don't understand," he said, confused. "What's this all about?"

Schuyler bit her lower lip, stalling. "I already told you—"

"No, you didn't," he insisted, trying to keep

his voice even. He didn't like games, especially not at his expense.

"Just hang on a little longer and you'll see what this is all about."

Everett sighed. "Well, since you've kidnapped me, I guess I don't have a choice."

"I didn't kidnap you," Schuyler informed him. "You got into the car of your own free will."

That's not how he saw it. "You just keep telling yourself that," he said. Laying his head back against the headrest, Everett closed his eyes. Running around and not getting much sleep was finally beginning to catch up with him. "Wake me whenever we get to wherever it is that we're going," he told her.

"We're here," Schuyler announced not five minutes later.

"Well, that didn't take long," Everett commented. Sitting up, he looked around as his sister got out of the car.

Schuyler had driven them to the Fortune Foundation.

Alert, not to mention annoyed, Everett glared

at his sister when he got out. "Hey, why are we here?"

"You'll find out," she said cheerfully.

Neither his mood nor the look that he was giving her over the hood of her car improved.

"Schuyler, just what the hell are you up to?" he demanded.

"You'll find out," his sister repeated. She gave him what she no doubt hoped was an encouraging look. "Just give it a few more minutes."

But Everett didn't move an inch. "And if I don't?"

"Then you'll never know how things might have turned out." When he still didn't move, Schuyler looked at him plaintively. "Do it for me, Everett. Please," she implored.

"Damn it, Schuyler, you owe me," Everett snapped, finally coming around the sporty red vehicle.

Schuyler inclined her head and gave him a wink. "We'll see."

Lila was engrossed in drawing up the following week's schedule for the volunteer doctors when Lucie walked into her office.

"Save whatever you're working on, Lila," Lucie told her. "I need your full, undivided attention right now."

Surprised by Lucie's serious tone, Lila looked up. "What's going on?"

Instead of answering her, Lucie looked over her shoulder and beckoned to someone. Just who was she summoning to Lila's office?

Totally stunned, Lila was immediately on her feet when she saw him.

Everett was the last person she'd expected to see here. After practically throwing him out of her house, she'd never thought she would see him again.

She fisted her hands, digging her knuckles into her desk to keep her knees from giving way.

She shot an angry look at her friend. "Lucie, what have you done?" she demanded.

"Saved two really nice people from a lifetime of loneliness and heartache," Lucie answered. Then she stepped out of the way, allowing a bewildered-looking Everett to enter Lila's office. But not before she gave a big grin and a high five to a well-dressed woman behind him.

Schuyler, Lila recognized.

Peering into the office around her brother, Schuyler declared, "I hereby officially call this intervention in session."

With that, she stepped away from the doorway.

Following her out, Lucie told the two people who were left in the room, "And don't come out until you've resolved this properly." And then she closed the door behind her.

"This your idea?" Lila asked Everett.

"Hell, no," he denied. "I think Schuyler cooked this up."

"Not without Lucie's help," Lila said accusingly. Furious, she let out a shaky breath. And then she turned toward Everett. She was furious. "You know you can leave," she told him.

"I know." Lord, but he had missed her, he thought now, looking at Lila. "But since I'm here...maybe we should talk."

"About what?" Lila wanted to know. "What is there left to say?" Restless, uneasy, she began to pace within the limited space. "I trusted you once and got my heart broken for my trouble."

Her accusation hurt. But this wasn't one-sided. "I could say the same thing," Everett countered.

Her eyes narrowed as she looked at Everett, stunned. "You?" she questioned. What was he talking about?

"Yes," he informed Lila. "I'd trusted you, too. Trusted that you'd be with me forever—and then you walked out. It wasn't easy for me after we broke up. I might have gone on with my studies—because that was what I was supposed to do—but there was this huge, empty, jagged hole in my chest where you used to be."

His dry laugh was totally mirthless as he continued. "I think I must have picked up the phone a hundred times that first year, wanting to call you and tell you about something that had happened in class or at the hospital, before I realized that I couldn't. That you wouldn't be there to answer the phone." His eyes met hers. "Nothing meant anything without you," he told her.

Lila stood there looking at him. The inside of her mouth felt like cotton and she struggled not to cry. She'd held her feelings in too long.

For thirteen years, to be exact. Now she could hold them in no longer.

"I still think about our baby all the time," she admitted.

Everett felt her words like a knife to his heart. More than anything, he wished he could go back in time to make things right. To do things differently. "Do you regret giving her up?"

"Yes," she answered so quietly, he had to strain to hear her. And then Lila took a deep breath. "No."

She blinked hard, telling herself she wasn't going to cry. Forbidding herself to shed a single tear. Tears were for the weak and she wasn't weak. She'd proven that over and over again.

"I know that our daughter has had a good life. The people who adopted her send me letters and photographs every once in a while, to let me know how she's doing." Lila smiled sadly. "Emma's a beautiful girl and she's doing really, really well in school."

Everett looked at her in surprise. He'd had no idea this was going on. "Her name is Emma? And you've stayed in contact with the family?" he asked.

Lila nodded. "Yes. Not knowing what was going on with Emma was killing me so it took a bit of doing but I managed to get in contact with the family that adopted her. Emma's parents are good people. They understood how hard it was for me to give up the baby. As a matter of fact, they're grateful to us for giving them what they call 'the most precious gift of all,'" Lila said. "Over the years, I've kept track of her through emails and pictures from her parents."

It was a lot for Everett to take in. Numerous questions rose in his head.

"How is she doing? What grade is she in now?" Everett asked.

"You actually want to know?" Lila asked him, astonished. "I mean, after the baby was born, you seemed really eager to put the whole incident behind you and forget about it. About her."

Her words stung, but he knew they were true. He'd been young and he'd just wanted to pretend that none of it had happened because it was easier to erase the guilt that way.

"I was," he admitted. "I'm not proud of it now, but it was the only way I could deal with it at the time, to just bury it and put it all totally out of my mind." Everett put his hands on her shoulders now, looking into Lila's eyes. "I'm sorry I wasn't more understanding, Lila. I didn't realize that you were hurting. I only knew that I was."

Lila struggled to wrap her mind around what he was telling her. She'd never suspected any of this. "You were hurting?"

Everett nodded. "She was my little girl, too," he told Lila.

"Oh, Everett, I wish you had told me," she cried.

So much time had been lost because of a failure to communicate. So much heartache could have been avoided if he had only verbalized his feelings to her.

If he'd just given her a clue…

"I wish I had told you, too," Everett said with all sincerity. And then he looked at her hopefully. "You wouldn't have a picture of Emma with you, would you?" he asked.

Lila opened up a drawer, took out her purse and pulled out her cell phone. She pressed the photo app and scrolled through a few photos until she came to the one she was looking for.

"This is Emma," she told Everett, holding out her phone to him.

Everett looked at the young girl on the screen. He could feel his heart swell as he stared at the image. Emma looked to be on the verge of her teen years and she had a mouth full of braces.

She was the most beautiful girl he had ever seen.

"She has your smile," he said, taking in every detail of the photo. And then he looked up at Lila. "I can't believe how beautiful our daughter is." With a sigh, he handed the phone back to Lila.

Lila closed her phone and put it back in her purse. "Emma's not our daughter anymore, Everett," she told him quietly.

Everett nodded. "Right. Have you ever seen her in person?"

Lila shook her head. "No. I wanted to, but I don't want to confuse Emma. One mother and father is enough for her right now at her age. Besides, her parents know how to get in contact with me. They have my cell number. Someday, when she's older, if Emma wants to meet me, they'll let me know and I'll be there in a heartbeat. But for right now, all I want is for Emma to grow up happy and well adjusted."

"You're a strong, brave woman, Lila," Everett told her with admiration. He hadn't realized until this moment just how strong and brave she really was.

Lila shrugged. "You do what you have to do in order to survive. And you make the best of the situation," she added. "The alternative is much too dark."

He nodded. "You're right. It is." He paused for a moment before looking at her and saying, "Would it surprise you if I told you that I think about Emma, too? That over the last few years, I've found myself thinking about her a lot. Wondering where she was, what she's doing. If she was happy. If she ever wondered about her birth parents and thought they—we—gave her up because we didn't love her."

"She knows we gave her up to give her a better life," Lila told him.

"You're just speculating," he said.

"No, I know that Emma knows that because her adoptive parents told me they told her that when she was old enough to begin asking questions."

Everett was quiet for a long moment. And when he finally spoke, what he said really surprised her. "I really wish I could meet our daughter."

It took Lila a moment to fully absorb what he had just said.

"Do you really mean that?" she asked Everett, astonished to hear him voice the same feelings that had been haunting her for years.

"Yes," he told her honestly. "I do."

She pressed her lips together, thinking over the feasibility of what he had just told her. "Well, I'm not sure how Emma's parents would feel about that, but I could certainly let them know that you're back in the picture and that you would like to meet Emma whenever it's convenient for them—and for her."

He nodded. It was a difficult situation all around and he fully understood that.

"I'd really appreciate that," he told her. He paused, trying to find the right words to convey what he wanted to say to her. "Lila…" Everett started, then stopped, his brain freezing up on him. This was a great deal harder than he'd anticipated.

"Yes?" she asked, wondering what else there was left for him to say. He'd already gladdened her heart by telling her that he not only thought about Emma, but actually wanted to meet her. That meant a great deal to her.

His eyes met hers. "Can you ever forgive me for not being there for you?" he asked softly.

Lila blinked. She could have been knocked over with the proverbial feather. Staring at Everett, she realized that he was being sincere.

"Oh Everett, I really wish I had known that you were hurting, too and that you felt the way you did. It would have helped me deal with everything that happened so much better." She smiled at him, fighting back tears again. "We really should have communicated more honestly with one another."

Everett stepped closer, letting himself do what he'd wanted to since he'd walked into this office. He enfolded Lila in his arms. "You're absolutely right. I should have talked with you, told you what I was feeling. But I just closed myself off, trying to deal with what was going on. I was blind and didn't realize that you were going through the same thing, too, and could have used my support." He'd been such a fool, Everett thought, regret riddling him. "Can you find it in your heart to forgive me?" he asked again.

Now that she knew that Everett had experienced the same doubts and emotions about their daughter that had haunted her, all of Lila's old feelings of anger and resentment vanished as if they had never existed. All Everett ever had to do was tell her what he'd gone through.

Forgiveness flooded her. "Yes, of course I can," she told him.

Relief mingled with love, all but overwhelming Everett. He kissed Lila, temporarily disregarding where they were and the fact that the people she worked with could easily look over and see what was happening.

And she kissed him back.

Everett forced himself to draw back. Still holding her in his arms, he looked down into her eyes. "From now on," he promised, "I'm putting all my cards on the table."

"Are you planning on playing solitaire or poker?" she asked Everett, a smile curving the corners of her mouth.

"Definitely not solitaire," he answered. "But any other game that you want. Oh, Lila, we've wasted much too much time and we'll never get any of that time back," he told her. His arms tightened around her. It felt so good to hold her against him like this. He felt he'd never let her go. "But we can have the future."

"And by that you mean...?" Her voice trailed off.

She wanted him to spell everything out so that there would be no more mix-ups, no more misunderstandings to haunt either one of them. She wanted to be absolutely certain that Everett was talking about what she *thought* he was talking about.

"I mean that I'm planning on being very clear about my intentions this time around. I know what I want," he told her, looking deep into her eyes. "All you need to do is say yes."

But she wasn't the same person she'd been thirteen years ago. She knew how to stand up for herself, how not to allow herself to be swept away.

She surprised him by telling Everett, "I never say 'yes' unless I know exactly what it is that I'm saying yes to."

"To this," Everett told her, pulling something out of his pocket. When he opened his hand, there was a big, beautiful heart-shaped diamond ring mounted on a wishbone setting in the center of his palm. He'd brought it with him for luck—and just in case.

Lila stared at it, momentarily speechless. When she raised her eyes to his face, she could barely speak. "Is that—?"

She couldn't bring herself to ask the question, because the moment she did—and he said no—a little of the magic would be gone. And she really couldn't believe that the ring she was looking at was the one she'd fallen in love with so many years ago.

But Lila discovered that she needn't have anticipated disappointment, because Everett nodded.

"Yes," he told her, pleased by her reaction, "it is. It's the one you saw through the window in that little out-of-the-way shop that day when we were back in college. You made me stand there while you made a wish and just stared at it, like it was the most beautiful thing you'd ever seen."

She smiled, remembering every detail. "I was being silly and frivolous," she admitted.

"No, you were being honest about your reaction," he corrected.

She continued looking at the sparkling diamond in his hand, completely mesmerized. "But how did you...?"

Everett anticipated her question and was way ahead of her. "After I dropped you off home, I doubled back to the store to buy the ring. The store was closed for the night by then, but I kept knocking on the door until the owner finally came down and opened it. Turns out that he lived above the store," he told her. "Anyway, I made him sell me the ring right then and there. I hung onto it, confident that I would give it to you someday." He smiled ruefully. "I just never thought it was going to take quite this long," he confessed.

Taking a deep breath, he held the ring up to her and said in a voice filled with emotion,

"Lila Clark, will you marry me? I promise if you say yes, I will never leave you again."

Lila could feel her heart beating so hard in her chest, she was certain it was going to break right through her ribs. The wish she'd made that day in front of the shop window was finally coming true.

"I don't plan to keep you on a leash," she told him, so filled with love she thought she was going to burst. "But yes, I will marry you."

Thrilled, dazed, relieved and experiencing a whole host of other emotions, Everett slipped the engagement ring on her finger.

The second he did, he swept her into his arms and kissed her again, longer this time even though he could see that they had attracted an audience. It didn't matter to him.

Lila's colleagues were watching them through the glass walls of her office and cheering them on, his sister and her cohort in front of the pack.

He looked down into Lila's eyes. "We can have more kids," he told her. "An entire army of kids if that's what you want. And they'll never want for anything. We can have that wonderful life that we used to just talk about having."

"A better one," she interjected.

"Absolutely," he agreed, hugging her to him again. "The sky's the limit," he promised. "But there's just one more thing."

"Oh?" Lila refused to be concerned. She'd been down that route and this was a brand-new route she was embarking on—with Everett beside her. She knew that she could face anything as long as he was with her. "What's that?"

"I don't want any more secrets between us," Everett said.

"Neither do I," Lila agreed wholeheartedly. "Is there something you need to tell me?"

"More than just you," Everett answered. "If we're going to start with a clean slate, there is something else I need to do."

Now he was beginning to really make her wonder, but she wasn't about to shrink away from his revelation. Because whatever it was, they would face it together. Conquer it together.

"Go ahead," Lila said, thinking that he was going to confess something serious to her.

Instead, Everett opened her office door and

called out, "Schuyler, Lucie, would you mind stepping back in here?"

The two women obligingly filed back into Lila's office.

"Okay," Schuyler said to her brother, "make your announcement, although we both saw you put that huge rock on Lila's finger so this is going to be a little anticlimatic."

"It's not what you think," Everett told his sister.

Schuyler exchanged looks with Lucie, obviously confused. "All right, enlighten us then," she said.

"I'm through sneaking around," he told his sister. "This is what we talked about when I first came to Austin, thinking I was picking you up to bring you home."

"What is he talking about?" Lucie asked, looking at Everett's sister.

Everett turned toward Lucie. "Lucie, I think it's time I told you who we really are. Or at least who we *think* we are."

Lucie looked from Everett to Lila, her brows furrowed. "Lila?"

But Lila shrugged, as mystified as Lucie was.

"I have no idea what he's talking about," she admitted.

Everett laced the fingers of one hand through Lila's hand as he went on to make his revelation. Nodding toward his sister, he told Lucie, "As you know, our last name is Fortunado."

Lucie waited for more. "Yes?"

"What you might not know, and I've recently come to find out—thanks to Schuyler's detective work—is that the Fortunado family might actually be descendants of Julius Fortune, Jerome Fortune's father," he added for clarity.

"You know," Lucie told Everett, a smile spreading across her face, "I'm not half surprised. With all of Jerome's illegitimate offspring coming to light lately, it stands to reason he learned the art of seduction from his father." She reached out and placed a hand on Everett's shoulder. "In that case, I have some people I would *really* love for you to meet."

"People who could substantiate my suspicions?" Everett wanted to know.

"Oh, more than substantiate, I think," Lucie said with emphasis.

Instead of eagerly asking her friend to make

the meeting happen, the way Lila thought he would, Everett turned to look at her. She saw a wicked sparkle in his eyes. Her pulse instantly began to accelerate.

"That really sounds wonderful, Lucie, and I'd appreciate the introduction," he told her without so much as a glance her way. His eyes were solely on Lila. "But I'm afraid the meeting is going to have to wait for now."

"Oh? Why?" Lucie asked.

"Because," Everett began, raising Lila's hand to his lips and brushing a kiss lightly against her knuckles, "my fiancée and I have plans for this afternoon. Plans," he said, "starting right now. So if you'll please excuse us..."

The request was merely a formality. Everett was already leading Lila out of the office and toward the hallway and the elevator beyond. He was vaguely aware of Schuyler's squeal of joy behind them and the sound of Lucie's laughter as she applauded.

All that and more blended into the background and then faded away as he stepped into the elevator car with Lila. They had a lot of catching up to do. And he planned to start this minute by taking her into his arms and kissing her as the elevator doors closed, locking the rest of the world out.

* * * * *

LET'S TALK

Romance

For exclusive extracts, competitions
and special offers, find us online:

f facebook.com/millsandboon

⊙ @millsandboonuk

🐦 @millsandboon

Or get in touch on 0844 844 1351*

For all the latest titles coming soon,
visit millsandboon.co.uk/nextmonth